Evolution, Me & Other Freaks of Nature

Robin Brande

Alfred A. Knopf ⟍ New York

THIS IS A BORZOI BOOK PUBLISHED BY ALFRED A. KNOPF

Published in the United States by Alfred A. Knopf,
an imprint of Random House Children's Books,
a division of Random House, Inc., New York.

www.randomhouse.com/teens

Educators and librarians, for a variety of teaching tools,
visit us at www.randomhouse.com/teachers

Library of Congress Cataloging-in-Publication Data
Brande, Robin.
Evolution, me, and other freaks of nature / Robin Brande. — 1st ed.
p.   cm.
SUMMARY: Following her conscience led high school freshman Mena to clash with her parents and former friends from their conservative Christian church, but might result in new friendships and more when she stands up for a teacher who refuses to include "Intelligent Design" in lessons on evolution.
ISBN 978-0-375-84349-5 (trade) — ISBN 978-0-375-94349-2 (lib. bdg.)
[1. Evolution—Fiction. 2. Conduct of life—Fiction. 3. Interpersonal relations—Fiction. 4. High schools—Fiction. 5. Schools—Fiction. 6. Christian life—Fiction. 7. Blogs—Fiction.] I. Title.
PZ7.B73598Evo 2007
[Fic]—dc22
2006034158

Printed in the United States of America

August 2007

10   9   8   7   6   5   4   3   2   1

First Edition

For Amanda and Matthew

Nothing is easier than to admit in words the truth of the universal struggle for life.

—Charles Darwin, *The Origin of Species*

One

I knew today would be ugly.

When you're single-handedly responsible for getting your church, your pastor, and every one of your former friends and their parents sued for millions of dollars, you expect to make some enemies. Fine.

It's just that I hoped my first day of school—of *high school,* thank you, which I've only been looking forward to my entire life—might turn out to be at least slightly better than eating live bugs. But I guess I was wrong.

I knew I'd be seeing some of these people today, but in first period already? And it has to be none other than my former best friend and the pastor's daughter—two of the people who have cause to hate me the most.

Having Teresa and Bethany in English might not be so bad if they'd just ignore me, but at the start of class when Mr. Kuhlman called, "Mena Reece," and I croaked out my "Here," Teresa had to turn her blond, spiky head around and shoot me the Look of Death, and I got that combined feeling of needing to throw up and possibly pee my pants.

Think positive. Think positive.

Why didn't my parents let me transfer? There are plenty of charter schools around, or they could have sent me to live with my aunt in Wyoming or with strangers in Alaska for all I care. But I know they want to see me punished. They pretend they've forgiven me, but I know deep down inside they hate me for writing that letter, just like everybody else.

It's only been half an hour, and already I can tell this is going to be the worst day of my life. I don't know why I'm so surprised. I knew seeing everyone today would be hard. It's only been a month since they were all served with the lawsuit, and even though I've gotten plenty of hate e-mails and phone messages since then, it's not the same as having to deal with these people in person.

I just didn't realize I'd be so scared. It's pathetic. What do I have to be afraid of? My conscience is clear. I didn't do anything wrong.

No, correction: I did the right thing. And someday the truth shall set me free.

Just not, apparently, today.

Two

Okay, at least second period wasn't so bad.

Maybe the only good thing about going to New Advantage High School (motto: "Let brilliance find you"—whatever that's supposed to mean) is they count yoga as PE. Also archery, tai chi, and kickboxing. But I'm glad I picked yoga. If ever a girl needs an hour between English and biology to chill out and breathe deeply and try to prevent her oncoming heart attack, that's me. Plus, I don't know a single person in my yoga class, for which I am truly grateful.

I wasn't sure my parents would let me take yoga. Pastor Wells was on this funk last year about how chanting during yoga or meditation is idol worship, because you're focused on a word or an image that isn't God and you're basically praying to it. He said the only acceptable way to meditate is to picture the Lord in front of you, his arms wide, a gentle smile on his face. Some women from the church even started their own class to teach us how to do it.

So this morning while our teacher, Missy, led us through the *pranas* and the *asanas*, I thought about Jesus the whole time. I pictured us on a hillside together, lying back on the grass while his flock grazed all around us.

I talked Jesus's ear off, but he smiled and let me go on. And when I had unloaded everything that was on my mind, he gave me a hug and called me Little Sister and told me everything will be all right.

It will, won't it? It felt so good to believe it.

Toward the end of class, Missy taught us some posture that I swear can only come in handy if you ever want to shave your own back. But our reward for pretzeling was that for the last twenty minutes of class she let us lie on our mats with our eyes closed, thinking our most peaceful thoughts.

I am in the woods, beside a calm, serene lake. The birds are singing. I can smell the pine. I am completely invisible. No one can find me. I've never heard of Denny Pierce.

And then the bell rang. Happy time was over.

I dressed as boring as I could today—plain jeans, a faded black T-shirt—hoping it would help hide me somehow. Right. As if I could walk even two steps down the hall without someone I know recognizing me and giving me the total Hairy Eyeball.

I kept my head down and plowed through, and had almost made it to my third-period biology class without bodily harm when someone hip-checked me into the wall.

I turned to see my former—don't know what to call him, really. Crush? Pre-boyfriend? The guy I was stupid enough to like last year and thought I might actually go out with once I'm allowed to date?—snickering and snuffling to himself. Yeah, Adam, that's so impressive. People must think you're really cool for tackling some girl you outweigh by a hundred pounds.

But I didn't say anything, of course. Just mumbled, "Don't," and hurried into class. Way to stick up for yourself, Mena. You showed him.

And then as if having Adam in that class isn't enough, guess who else? Teresa, of course, because apparently having her in English just isn't enough torture. For all I know, she's probably in all my classes except yoga, and tomorrow she'll transfer into that, too, just to make sure I'm living my own personal hell.

I grabbed a seat as far away from her as possible, but Teresa still managed to throw me a look like would I do everyone a favor and just die.

If the day keeps going like this, I might.

Three

Right before biology started, this enormous senior-looking guy came into the room and handed our teacher, Ms. Shepherd, a venti Starbucks. She clasped her hands together like God had answered her prayer, then scrounged in her purse for the cash. She thanked the giant and dismissed him, then held the cup to her nose, closed her eyes, sniffed through the lid, and finally took her first sip. It was like her own personal yoga moment.

I had nothing else to do but watch her, since the last thing I wanted to do was make eye contact with any of the other people filing into the room. What a nightmare. Not only Adam and Teresa, but fully half of that class are people from my church.

My *ex*-church. My parents still go there, but Pastor Wells let it be known that I'm no longer welcome. Fine. As if I could stand being around those people anymore anyway.

So I stared at Ms. Shepherd instead. She's kind of pretty, in a nerdy smart-looking way, if that makes any sense. She's short and a little fleshy, but not really fat—more like comfortable. She has tan skin and dark eyes and messy black hair. She wears these kind of funky/nerdy black horn-rim glasses that you'd choose for an actress if she were going to play a science teacher in a movie.

But you wouldn't pick those clothes. First of all, her shoes were beyond ugly—all scuffed and blocky and hideous. And her clothes were so wrinkled it's like she'd slept in them. When I was little I used to sleep in my clothes before the first day of school, I was so excited, but I doubt teachers feel that way. I think Ms. Shepherd might just be a slob.

I kept on hearing my name. I swear I'm not paranoid—people really were talking about me. I heard a few choice words I wish I hadn't.

I reached into my backpack and started taking stuff out, and meanwhile secretly counted how many of them were in the room. Fourteen. Fourteen people from my church youth group. Nine of them being sued by Denny Pierce's parents, thanks to me. I was going to be sick.

The bell rang. Ms. Shepherd stayed where she was, rear end perched against her desk, eyes closed, Starbucks gripped lovingly in her hand while she enjoyed just a few extra moments of caffeine bliss. Then her eyes jolted open as if the beans had just kicked in.

"Okay, then, people, here's the story," she began. "I don't grade on a curve. I don't reward mediocrity. Your grades will depend on test scores, lab work, class participation, and a special project due at the end of the semester.

What's the special project, you ask? See me after class if you want a jump on it. Otherwise wait to find out with the masses."

She picked up her roster and forged ahead. "I will be assigning your lab partners. No, you may not switch. Jeremy Agee?"

Startled, Jeremy answered. "H-ere."

"A raised hand will do," Ms. Shepherd said before speeding on.

My stomach tensed. Here was my first real test of bravery. I'd know with the next name she called whether Ms. Shepherd was going down the roster by twos. If so, chances were she'd see Mena Reece and Teresa Roberts and think we'd make a great pair, and wouldn't realize she had just mixed holy water with acid.

Not that I'm holy water. But Teresa is what she is.

But Ms. Shepherd went the creative route and paired Jeremy Agee with Juan Zamora, and to my bottomless gratitude, she paired me with a person named Casey Connor.

I was so relieved it wasn't Teresa, I forgot to see who raised a hand at the same time I did.

I scanned the room, not sure if I was searching for a boy or a girl. Could be either these days. In fifth grade there were two Hunters—a boy and a girl—and at church there are four Aidens of various genders. Mena could be a boy, I suppose, except that I'm named for some gnarled-up old Czechoslovakian grandmother my mom grew up next door to and loved, apparently, more than her own

8

grandmothers, who had decent names like Elizabeth and Rose.

Ms. Shepherd zipped through the list, then told us to find our partners.

I stayed put—no way was I leaving the safety of my chair. I kept my eyes to myself and hoped whoever my lab partner was, he or she wouldn't mind searching for me.

A boy about my size, with pale skin and dark eyebrows and curly black hair, came toward me. "Hallo, Miss Reece?" he asked in a British accent, tipping an imaginary hat. I nodded, a little stunned. "Pleasure. Casey Connor." He shook my hand, then stuffed his backpack underneath the chair beside me and sat down.

I was just processing how cool it was to have a lab partner from England when suddenly Casey dropped the accent and said in his normal voice, "Don't worry, I've got the special project all worked out. Unless you have an idea, which is fine—let's put them all on the table. But one way or another you and I *are* going to win this year. No question."

I had no idea what he was talking about. It's like I'd barged in on someone else's conversation. Before I could sound as stupid as I felt, Ms. Shepherd saved me by clapping for attention.

She took another deep sip of coffee, then scanned each of our faces like we had all been brought in for questioning. "Listen up. You need to understand something before we begin. I love science—love it. I mean LOVE IT."

9

There was silence for a second, then a few kids snickered. Adam Ridgeway said, "Okaaayy . . ."

Casey whispered, "This is going to be great!"

In that moment I knew: my lab partner is a total geek.

"I tell you that," Ms. Shepherd continued, "because I know that sitting in front of me right now are some of the future scientists of America. I say to you, welcome. WELCOME. You are the people whose curiosity will uncover the riches of our universe. You are the ones who will show us what greatness the human mind is capable of. YOU are the people who will save us from ourselves. Let's give you all a round of applause."

She and Casey were the only ones clapping at first. Then some of the rest of us joined in, a little tentatively. I looked over at my former comrades, off in their herd whispering and laughing at Ms. Shepherd. Which only made me clap all the harder.

Ms. Shepherd lifted her Starbucks in salute. "All right, then. No time to lose. Let's go make some science."

She grabbed a burlap sack from behind her desk and cruised around the room. Next thing I know, there's a potato sitting on my desk.

"You have to share," Ms. Shepherd told us. "And no snacking."

"What's this for?" some boy asked.

"To make you brilliant," Ms. Shepherd answered. "Just like it says in the brochure."

Casey Connor picked up our potato. "I did this in camp once. The potato actually *flies*." Not sure if he was serious or not.

Ms. Shepherd returned to the front of the room. Then she spun around, her back to us, and asked, "What color is my shirt?" She was wearing a jacket over it, so the answer wasn't obvious.

"Red," a girl called out.

"No," Ms. Shepherd snapped.

"Green," someone else tried.

"No."

A few more attempts before Ms. Shepherd gave up and turned around. "Puce. My shirt is puce."

"Puke?" said Adam (always the funny man) (not). It dawned on me suddenly that if Ms. Shepherd had been going alphabetically by twos, I would have ended up with him instead of Teresa, which would have been equally horrifying. I said a silent thank-you for Casey.

"Puce," Ms. Shepherd repeated. "Dark red."

"I said 'red'!" complained the girl who had.

"Not 'red,' " Ms. Shepherd said. " 'Red' is general— 'red' is boring. 'Puce' is specific. These are the distinctions we scientists must make. Something isn't simply 'green' or 'orange' or 'smelly'—"

That cracked people up, although they weren't laughing *with* her, I don't think.

"When you're a scientist, you deal in specifics. If I say I love you"—she pointed to a chubby boy hunched over his desk in back—"then I should be able to say I love you to this certain degree and temperature and height and width. Follow?"

No one followed. And the chubby guy looked ready to bolt.

11

"So with your potato, I want you to treat that like it's the most beloved thing you've ever had in front of you in your life—"

"I love you!" Adam told his potato. *I can't believe I used to like that guy.*

Ms. Shepherd ignored him. "—like it's gold or sapphires or your favorite cat. Follow? Or like it's the man or woman of your dreams—"

"What are you *talking* about?" Teresa interrupted in her snottiest, most defiant way. *I used to delight in being around her when she did things like that. I could be the good girl hiding in the background while my best friend took charge of being dangerous.*

"I'm talking about observation," answered Ms. Shepherd, readjusting the glasses that had slipped down her nose. "I'm talking about precision. I'm talking about leaving behind all those broad generalities you teenagers speak in and finally getting down to some specifics.

"You." She pointed to Lara Donaldson. (*Church. Hates me.*) "Give me your potato."

Lara so willingly did.

Ms. Shepherd removed her glasses and stared bare-eyed at the potato. "Not young, not old—"

"Just right," Adam joked.

"Not for the scientist to judge," Ms. Shepherd said. "Color?"

She pointed to Lara.

"Uh, brown?" Lara answered, in a tone that clearly meant, "Uh, duh?"

"Wrong. Is my shirt red? It's puce. What color is this potato?"

I ventured a try. "Tan?"

"Not tan, so much," Ms. Shepherd said. "Too dark for tan. Anyone?"

Casey Connor held up his textbook and pointed to the color of the title. "Biology brown."

Ms. Shepherd put her glasses back on and looked from the book back to the potato. "All right, we'll accept that answer for now. Heads up." She tossed the potato back to a startled Lara, who fumbled it and had to dive under her desk to keep it from escaping like the meatball in "On Top of Spaghetti."

"Got it?" Ms. Shepherd asked. "You have two class periods. I want to know everything—*ev-ery-thing*—you can tell me about your potato. No making up funny names for it or family history—let me stop you right there." She looked pointedly at Adam. "We want facts—always facts."

She reached behind her onto her desk and lifted a mysterious, misshapen package. "Team with the best and most descriptions wins *this*."

Before we could even process whether or not we'd even want whatever that thing was—and I'm still not sure, since it was the weirdest-shaped package I've ever seen—Ms. Shepherd shooed us with her free hand. "Go. Go. Make science."

Well, no one can get right to work after a weird performance like that. It requires a little chatter. The room was all abuzz.

I blew out a breath and looked at Casey.

He must have seen I was a little skeptical about Ms. Shepherd, because the first thing he said was, "She's a genius. You should Google her. She has about twenty published papers in the top scientific journals. She's world-renowned."

"For what?"

"Anthropological mathematics and dynamism."

I nodded as if I understood what he'd just said.

"Just kidding. Cellular biology with some physics on the side. Anything from string theory to genomic mutations to quantum mechanics."

"Oh. Wow." As if I understood any of that, either.

"So what'd you think?" Casey asked.

"About . . ."

"Ms. Shepherd. Pretty great, huh?"

"Yeah. Pretty great." Whatever. I think my lab partner might be as psycho as my teacher.

Ms. Shepherd was walking around the room, making sure we were getting to know our potatoes, so we had to keep it down.

"We're winning that prize," Casey said, gesturing toward the mysterious package on Ms. Shepherd's desk. "Make no mistake."

"What do you think it is?"

"Who cares? It's a *prize*. That's all we need to know. Bottom line."

"Oh, you're one of those," I joked, but really it didn't bother me. I'm not a competitive person by nature, but maybe I could use a little push these days. Besides, working hard in school might be the only thing I have right now to take my mind off my life.

Against my will I glanced over at Teresa. Something about her bleached-out head always draws the eye—that, and the fact that she thinks it's funny to mix religion and sleaze. Today she's wearing these shockingly low-cut jeans I can't believe her parents ever let her buy, along with a red (devil red—how's that for specific, Ms. Shepherd?) *Jesus Freak* T-shirt about two sizes too small to make sure everyone notices her boobs. Guess that'll bring the guys to church.

She was laughing with her lab partner, Kelsey Dunbar (also church, also hates me), and I could just tell from the way Teresa's mouth looked—cruel and snide—that she was saying something mean right at that moment, either about me or about Ms. Shepherd.

"Yeah," I told Casey, "winning sounds good."

Four

Which brings us to now—lunch.

I never, ever, EVER thought I'd be sitting alone in the cafeteria on my first day of high school. Ever.

It's so noisy. There are so many kids here. And even though I know a lot of them, it's not as many as I thought. I guess it's possible that there are hundreds of people here who haven't heard of me, don't care what I did—might even be horrified at the whole story and the way I'm being treated and instantly take my side. Those people are my friends. Now I just have to find them.

In the meantime, I'll look as busy as possible writing in this notebook, eating my turkey and Swiss, unpeeling my banana—all these important activities that simply keep me too occupied to look up and notice that I'm alone.

I bought this notebook on a whim. I think it was meant for younger kids, but I don't care. I might just love it. Like loving my potato.

It has a red cover—no, more of a pinkish burgundy—and it's made of some kind of fabric (sorry, Ms. Shepherd, don't know what kind) that's fuzzy like short-cropped fur, and I know it's sick, but I have this incredible urge to rub it against my cheek right now for a little bit of comfort, like the old days of rubbing my favorite blanket against my face while I sucked my thumb.

I don't see that Casey guy anywhere. Maybe he has a different lunch. I do see Teresa and Bethany and the whole host of holy Christians, half of whom have done far worse things than people act like I have, and yet they still get to wear their *I ♥ Jesus* T-shirts to school, and no one would dare challenge them.

If I showed up in my *Jesus Freak* T-shirt or my *WWJD* bracelet, they'd stone me before I got through the door.

Must keep busy.

Let's make a to-do list.

1. Find some friends. No, let's keep it simple: Find one friend. Cling to her like static.
2. Stop caring what anyone thinks. If they're talking about you, so what? You know you did the right thing, so hold your head high. I mean it.
3. Find a club to join. There are lots of kids at this school and lots of interesting things to do besides go to church group every other night. Expand your horizons.
4. Do great in school this year. I mean not just your usual great, but exceptionally great. Shove their noses in it.

5. Try to make the parents like you again. There has to be a way.
6. Either learn to eat alone and not care or find someplace else to go at lunch. Library? Parking lot? (No, too many stoners and smokers, I'm sure.) Always have a book to read. Always carry this notebook. Appear busy at all times.
7. Stop obsessing about all of this. If you move on, others will, too. Honest.
8. Do something better with your hair besides this ponytail.
9. Grow out your nails.
10. Stop worrying.

Busy, busy, busy. That's me, writing away, so busy I can't notice that Teresa is walking straight toward me.

Five

It's unnatural to sweat as much as I just did, just from a thirty-second conversation.

It's the first time Teresa and I have talked face to face since the lawsuit got filed. I've gotten plenty of e-mails from her in the last few weeks telling me what a *b-i-t-c-h* I am, but it's not like hearing it in person.

"So," Teresa said.

I pretended not to hear.

"How's it feel, traitor?"

I just kept my head down and pretended to keep eating, as if I could swallow anything.

She picked up my banana peel and tossed it on top of my sandwich. "I said, how's it feel, *bitch*?"

She leaned over the table and grabbed my wrist. And twisted it.

I held my breath. I didn't make a sound.

Her face was so close to mine I could smell her gum.

"So what's it like to be the most hated person in this school? Bet you're glad you opened your big fat mouth."

She stopped twisting, but still held on to my wrist.

"I thought we were friends. How could you do that to me? What were you thinking?"

I couldn't look at her. I couldn't breathe.

"Answer me!"

My hand was numb. All of me was.

Teresa straightened up and tossed my wrist away. "You're pathetic, you know that? You're nothing. You might as well be dead." She slapped her hand over her mouth. "Oh, whoops, did I say something bad? Mommy gonna sue me?"

She leaned toward me again. She smelled like cinnamon and hair gel. "Stay away from me. I mean it. You understand?"

I didn't move, didn't make a peep. I wouldn't have put it past her to slap me if I did.

"I'm talking to you, Judas! Do you hear me?"

I knew people were staring at us, but there was nothing I could do about it. I just had to sit there and take it.

"You're pathetic." She picked up my banana peel and threw it at my chest.

It's still there, the peel. It's sitting on my lap. I haven't touched it. I haven't done anything since Teresa stalked off except go back to writing in this notebook. I am such a coward. I feel sick. I'm such a baby. I have to be stronger than this, or I'll never make it past today. Keep writing. Don't let them see you shaking. Write, write, write.

It's just that HOW AM I SUPPOSED TO DEAL WITH ALL THIS??? After everything they did to Denny, now they get to act like I'M the bad guy? Just because I tried to fix it? I didn't write that letter because I wanted anyone to get in trouble. I did it because I was trying to be a good person, even if it was too late.

There's the bell. Thank GOD, and I mean that literally. Please let this day hurry up and be over.

At least please don't let it get any worse.

Six

Home—thank goodness. I wish I could figure out some way of never having to leave my room again. I'm beginning to understand the appeal of home schooling. Not that it would work so well in my case, since my parents can't exactly stand me right now, either. I wonder if you can take high school over the internet.

At least my afternoon wasn't so bad. French, world civ, and algebra—and Teresa wasn't in a single one of those. Yay! Lara's in French, Bethany Wells is in world civ, and there are three people who hate me in algebra, but I think I can take all that. As long as I know I'm always going to be done with Teresa by lunch.

I'm up here pretending to do homework (which I actually do need to do) (later). Mom is in the kitchen making something for the church bake sale tonight and trying to forget she ever gave birth to me. Just when I think she can't get any madder, she'll have a bad day like today, when she gets another call from one of the parents who got sued, and it reminds her all over again how much she hates me.

Not that she would ever say that to my face, but come on—it's so obvious. She barely says four words to me anymore. I'm sure she'd prefer that from now on I stay in my room after school and just work, work, work. Anything, as long as I'm not having fun.

She doesn't know that what I've really been doing since I got home is looking up Ms. Shepherd on the internet, deleting a bunch of nasty e-mails from my former friends, obsessing over every single detail of my day, and finally thinking a little about Casey Connor, although I'm not really sure why.

It's just that he is kind of funny. We had about twenty minutes left of class to spend with our potato today, and Casey started by switching back to his British accent and badgering it with questions.

"Tell me, Mr. Potato—" He lifted the spud to his ear. "What's that? Sorry, Mzzzz Potato. Enjoying the States, are you? Out to see the grandspuds in Idaho? Been shot from any cannons lately?"

Ms. Shepherd was doing the rounds, and as she came near us Casey switched to a very serious (American) voice and started rattling off terms like "circumference" and "nucleotides" and "swatchnoid." I nodded studiously and copied them on our work sheet.

After a few moments Casey looked around to make sure no one else was listening, then whispered like a British detective, "Potato shows signs of trauma, possibly made by shovel or trowel."

"I was thinking a spade," Ms. Shepherd said behind us. "Facts, people, facts."

Casey blushed puce.

When the coast was clear, he went back to talking to our potato. "That's right, you're the prettiest spud in here. Don't even look at the others. They're all so jealous of you." He covered the potato's ears—I guess—and whispered to me, "She thinks she's fat. Tell her." He thrust the potato in my face.

"All the other potatoes are much fatter," I said, patting her on the head. "And you have a much better personality."

I felt kind of stupid, but kind of not. The truth is, it was fun to play around. It's been too long since anyone wanted to just hang out with me and goof off.

"Good," Casey said, slamming the potato to his desk. "Now let's chop this thing to bits."

I should get to my homework soon. I actually have a fair amount to do. But I'm guessing I'll have plenty of time tonight. I don't imagine Mom will call me down to help with dinner—she hasn't for the past month, so why start now? It's a weird sort of punishment, not having to set the table or peel the carrots or whatever anymore, but I know what she means by it. She doesn't want me around her right now. She's still too upset.

And then there's my father's inability lately to ever look me in the eye. I say something, and if I'm lucky he mumbles something back, but he won't grace me with a look.

Good times.

Look, let's start over. There has to be a better way of handling all of this.

First of all, I can't let these people get to me anymore. Everything happens for a reason, right? Things are awful and ugly right now, but maybe they had to be that way for me to ever break free. Because I knew last year what these people were doing was wrong, but I just didn't have the guts to do anything about it. So now God has taken care of that for me by getting me kicked out of the church. I should be grateful. Really.

Second, I need to focus all of my energies on something positive. So starting right now, I am going to throw myself into my schoolwork. I am going to get straight A's this year and win every award there is to win—including Ms. Shepherd's weird potato prize. Maybe that will prove to my parents that I'm not a total reject as a child. If I can't fix what I've already done, at least I can do better in the future.

Plus, concentrating on school will keep me completely occupied, and my former friends will have to notice they haven't turned me into a quivering hunk of weeniness just because they've ostracized me.

So:

1. Start doing my homework the second I get home from school every day.
2. Take on any extra-credit projects any teacher offers.
3. Work extra hard in the subjects that aren't my best, like math and science.
4. Win every single prize and award there is to win.
5. Get straight A's this year and every year.

6. Get better grades than Teresa or anyone else.
7. Make a bunch of new friends who are smarter and more fun than the ones I used to have.

That ought to rub their noses in it. Vengeance is mine, sayeth the Lord, but sometimes it's hard not to get a jump on it yourself.

Seven

Day two of Her Miserable Life.

Started with a lovely scene at the start of Mr. Kuhlman's class, when I overheard Bethany tell Teresa, "My dad said to meet at our house tomorrow night."

Great. A meeting at Pastor Wells's house means something new is in the works. What fire and brimstone does he plan on unleashing this time? Is he really going to start some new campaign even though the Pierces are probably going to win millions of dollars against him and the church because of the last one? What is he thinking?

But it's not my problem this time. I am so glad. I never realized how wonderful it would feel to be free of the whole thing. I'm sorry my parents might lose their business over this, but I'm not sorry for speaking up. Somebody had to say something.

So while Teresa and Bethany huddled together, and Teresa made sure to speak clearly and loudly so I could overhear them, I just kept my head down and waited for the bell. And the whole time I felt like shouting,

WHO CARES? Because I really don't. I've participated in my last act of Christian aggression, thank you. I am cured for life.

Bethany glanced over at me a few times, like she felt guilty I could overhear.

Well, Bethany should feel guilty, but not for that. I have to believe that in her heart of hearts she knows she's as responsible as her father is for this whole mess. It may have been Pastor Wells's idea to start that whole campaign at our school, but Bethany's the one who took charge of carrying it out. I'm sure her intentions were noble, knowing her, but she should have thought of the consequences.

Thank God the bell for class finally rang and Teresa had to shut up.

Today we started *A Tale of Two Cities,* by Charles Dickens. Mr. Kuhlman has this great books-on-tape kind of voice, and he read aloud from the first few pages while we followed along. "It was the best of times, it was the worst of times. . . ."

You said it, Dickens. Except for the "best of times" part.

Eight

Casey said, "Let's start with the least obvious facts. Then work backwards."

All around us, people were weighing their potatoes, fondling their potatoes, measuring them, sniffing them—it was a potato orgy.

But Casey and I were Scientific.

Casey brought a whole bag of stuff from home today: baseball, softball, cantaloupe, paint-chip color chart, Crayola box (the megabox, to make sure we matched the colors exactly), printouts from the internet, some measuring tool called calipers ("I wasn't sure if she'd have any in here," he explained. I nodded, since I wasn't sure, either—what a caliper is, I mean), an awl ("I'm probably not supposed to bring that on campus—probably counts as a sharp"), a paperback science fiction novel titled *Gaunt Messenger* ("There's a great sequence in there where they live on nothing but potatoes for eight months—we should throw in a few lines from that")—who knows what else. I was simply amazed. I only brought my fuzzy notebook.

"We're going to compare and contrast the potato to all these other things," Casey explained about the baseball and softball and cantaloupe. "Distill and eliminate all the common properties."

I kept nodding. What else could I do? Some people have Science Brain, some don't. Compare and contrast that.

We found an unoccupied corner of the room and got to work. We were in the middle of adding dried figs to one side of the scale (think Teresa's partner brought dried figs? Sucka) when Ms. Shepherd came over to us, watched for a second, took a sip of her Starbucks (delivered by the same giant—she must have a contract with him), nodded, and moved on without a word. Maybe she thinks we're geniuses. Maybe she thinks we're freaks. In either case, takes one to know one.

Because I looked her up on the internet, all right. Wow. Undergrad at Brown University, PhD at Harvard. She has her own website, with a blog she updates every week or so. The last entry talked about some trip she took to Bermuda over the summer, and how they drive on the left side of the road there, and she kept turning her head the wrong way to look for oncoming traffic and almost got mowed down by a moped. She also wrote something about a guy named "Herc," and she wasn't sure if that was short for "Hercules," but she doubted it. She didn't really say how she knew him.

She was there for a science conference. She won an award for some discovery or research paper or something— it wasn't too clear. She was pretty modest about it. She just said she had a hard time dressing up for the awards dinner because the last time she wore high heels she was about twelve, but her colleagues assured her this was a heels event. But by the time the emcee announced her name, her feet hurt so badly she just walked up to the podium barefoot. She didn't think anyone noticed.

I asked Casey if he read that.

"Sure. You should have seen one of the ones from June. She picked up some rash while camping in the Adirondacks, and then she took in her own skin and blood samples to a lab and it turned out to be some new parasite no one's ever heard of before." Casey snapped his fingers. "Another discovery, just like that. She's brilliant."

"How long have you been reading her blog?"

"Three years."

"Why? Two-point-five," I added, giving him the caliper measurement of one of the potato's eyes.

"My sister had her freshman year. We're both big fans."

I can't imagine being a "big fan" of a teacher I'd never even had. Casey must not get out much.

"So why do you think she's teaching high school, then?" I asked. "I mean, if she's so brilliant."

"Check her FAQs. Her high school biology teacher is the one who turned her on to science. She feels it's her mission to pass it on. You forgot that one." Casey pointed to a blemish on the surface of the potato. "Looks like the Big Dipper."

I traced it onto our paper next to my other sketches of strange features on the potato's surface. One of them looked like half of Mickey Mouse's head.

"We need to do a summary," Casey said. "Eyes, bumps, discolorations—"

But Ms. Shepherd called time. Hard to believe how quickly it had passed. Guess the minutes just slip away when you're loving your potato like we were.

"I'll review these tonight," Ms. Shepherd said of our reports. She held up the oddly shaped package once more. "Tomorrow, some lucky team . . ." She smiled mysteriously. "Hope you can all sleep tonight."

"You know we're going to win," Casey told me as we gathered our books. "Whatever it is, we'll split it."

"It was all you," I pointed out. "I couldn't have thought of any of that."

He switched to British. "Don't be so modest. I depend on you, Watson."

I was working on something witty to say back when suddenly someone rammed me from behind and gouged my pelvis against the desk.

I spun around in time to see Teresa keep on walking toward the door. She looked quite pleased with herself. Another slam and run just like Adam's in the hall. Must have been last week's Sunday-school lesson.

"Excuse you," Casey called after her. Teresa didn't even bother turning around.

"Well," Casey said. "Obviously a close personal friend."

"Yeah, right."

"You okay?"

I nodded. It was so humiliating, letting him see me get bullied like that—and me not doing anything about it.

The least I could do was look brave. I resisted rubbing the spot where my desk had hit.

"So, what's Miss Q-Tip have against you?"

I don't know why that never occurred to me before. Probably because you don't make up a mean nickname for someone until she stops being your best friend. "Long story."

"Once upon a time, Q-Tip and Mena . . ." He rolled his hand in the air to prompt me onward.

I shook my head. "Trust me, you don't want to know."

"Then I'll just have to make something up. She stole your identity, poisoned your dog—"

"Casey—"

"—drugged you at a sleepover party and let someone tattoo a pirate ship on your bum."

"Bingo. How'd you know?"

"Same thing happened to me once."

If I hadn't been so tired from the whole Teresa thing this morning—two, count them, two class periods of fun—I might have joked around a little longer. But I felt like taking a rest.

"Well . . . I gotta go." I shouldered my backpack and started for the door.

Ms. Shepherd was up front, browsing through our potato reports while she waited for her next class. "*Gaunt Messenger*," she said to Casey. "Interesting."

"Oh. Yeah." He glanced at me, then suddenly seemed in a big hurry to gather his stuff.

"One of his best," Ms. Shepherd said.

"Yeah. Thanks." Casey had a weird look on his face. He headed for the door.

Now it was my turn to be curious. I followed him into the hall. "So?"

"What?"

"What was that about?"

"I don't know," Casey said. "I guess she just likes that book."

"Then why did you say 'thanks'? Like you had something to do with it?"

"It's . . . one of my dad's books. He wrote it."

"No way."

"Yeah. Well, see you tomorrow." Casey merged into hallway traffic and left me behind.

I turned to see Ms. Shepherd standing in her doorway.

"Didn't notice the name Connor on the cover?" she asked.

"Pardon?"

She clicked her tongue. "Better work on your powers of observation, Ms. Reece."

Nine

We won. I knew we would. Casey is too smart not to win. He says some of my ideas were pretty great, too, but trust me—it was all him.

I have to admit I felt a little smug this morning as the two of us went to the front of the room to claim our prize. I even sneaked a peek at Teresa and saw exactly what I wanted to see: Displeasure. Jealousy. Good. Suck on that.

And then Ms. Shepherd presented us with our trophy. Casey and I struggled to unwrap it.

"Good tape job, huh?" Ms. Shepherd said proudly. "Might want to use your teeth."

We didn't, so it took a while to unwrap, but finally what did our eyes behold?

A stuffed animal, and I don't mean stuffed as in cute and cuddly, pick it up at Toys "R" Us. I mean stuffed as in taxidermed.

Oh. My. Gosh.

Casey smiled like he'd just won fifty bucks.

It was a dead rabbit—no, not a rabbit—a freakish,

mutated, hideous bunny-like creature with antlers growing out of its head. It was a real dead animal—I felt its fur.

People craned out of their desks. "What the—" someone started to say.

"What is it, you ask?" said Ms. Shepherd. "Any guesses?"

Of course Casey would know. "It's a jackalope."

"Correct! Ding, ding, ding—a young man who knows his science. This, my friends, is indeed the mighty jackalope. Also known as deerbunny, killer rabbit, warrior rabbit, *Wolpertinger* in German. The result of crossbreeding between the Australian pygmy deer and the carnivorous European jackrabbit. May I borrow that?"

Casey handed her our prize and shot me a look of utter delight. I couldn't see what he was so pleased about—that thing was disgusting. There was no way I was ever touching it again.

"Note the sharp, vicious teeth," Ms. Shepherd said. "The elongated jackrabbit ears, the double-pronged antlers, the powerful hindquarters—"

"That's fake!" Jesse Pruitt shouted. (Church. Hates me.)

"What do you mean, fake?" Ms. Shepherd said. "It's as real as I am. You can see it, touch it—" She sniffed it and made a face. "Certainly smell it. It's right here where you can all observe it, right? So how can it not be real?"

"There's no such thing," Jesse said, but you could tell he wasn't so sure.

Ms. Shepherd turned to Casey. "What can you tell us about the jackalope, Mr. Connor?"

36

He quickly hid his smile and matched Ms. Shepherd's clinical tone. "They're found in New Mexico—specifically Santa Fe. I'm not sure where else."

"Ah, yes," Ms. Shepherd said. "Santa Fe does have a large population. Also Wyoming, Colorado, parts of Europe—more locations are discovered every year. Very good. We also know that their bite is extremely toxic, but curiously, their milk—"

"Their milk!" Adam protested.

Ms. Shepherd pointed to where the spigot must be. "Their milk is thought to have healing properties." She handed the jackalope back to Casey, who cradled the creature as gently as if it really were a sweet little living bunny. That guy has serious problems.

Ms. Shepherd reached behind us onto her desk, shifted aside a few science journals, and retrieved a small vial filled with white liquid. "This small amount costs about a thousand dollars on the open market."

"A thousand bucks?" Adam repeated skeptically. Now people were paying attention.

"Not surprising," Ms. Shepherd said. "It's very difficult to milk a jackalope without being bitten. People have died. I met a man whose forefinger was completely shriveled up from it—like an empty, rotten banana peel."

"Gross!" some girl said.

"I've been saving this for a while." Ms. Shepherd removed the rubber stopper on the vial. "But I noticed my throat has been getting a little scratchy." She made a kind of hacking noise to demonstrate. "This should fix it right up."

Ignoring the chorus of "ewwws," Ms. Shepherd tipped the contents of the vial into her Starbucks and gave it a swirl. While we watched in horror, she took a big swig of coffee, then licked her lips. "Hmm. Burns a little."

"Gross!" that girl repeated.

"You're crazy!" said Jesse.

Casey was trying so hard not to smile, it looked like it made his own lips hurt.

Ms. Shepherd took one more sip and cleared her throat. "Good. It's working already. Now, on to today's lesson."

She dismissed us and our prize—which I let Casey carry, since I wanted nothing to do with it, thank you—and we returned to our desks in back.

While Ms. Shepherd went over some of the findings in people's potato reports (who knew Lara had such a gift for potato sculpture? Ms. Shepherd called her up to exhibit her work), Casey leaned over and whispered, "I love her."

I whispered back, "Tell me the truth. Is that real?"

"Nope. Totally fake."

"What?" The kid in front of me turned around, so I waited and lowered my voice. "What, you mean the milk?"

"All of it—jackalopes. They're novelty items. I saw a bunch in a gift shop in Santa Fe once. They're hilarious."

"So she lied?" I asked.

"Yep."

"Wow." I've never met a teacher before who would pull a practical joke like that. I have to say, I admire her for it. I never could have done it with a straight face. "So you think she'll tell everyone? I mean, eventually?"

"I certainly hope not."

For the rest of class, while Ms. Shepherd talked about some article she'd read last night on the latest outbreak of the Ebola virus, I studied her with fresh interest. She's wacky, there's no doubt. But maybe wacky in a good way.

And to think Casey knew it was a joke the whole time and went along with it. All these straight-faced liars—I could learn a lesson from them. My life might really improve if I could just stop feeling so committed to the truth.

Toward the end of the period Ms. Shepherd gave us our homework assignment. "I need three scientifically proven facts about the jackalope. Papers are due tomorrow."

People groaned, of course, but Casey and I smiled at each other. This was going to be fun. Fact number one: fake.

All in all, it was a pretty great class. But of course Teresa couldn't resist ruining it for me.

Casey and I happened to walk out together, and Teresa was waiting.

"Love your prize, Mena." She tilted her head toward Casey. "Ahh, that's sweet—you made a new little gay friend already."

Casey looked as shocked as I was. That girl is evil—pure evil. I don't know why it surprises me anymore.

"He's not—" But that was all I could get out before my tongue froze up. How should I know what he is or isn't?

And what business is that of Teresa's? Why should she get to torment somebody new just because he's unfortunate enough to be my lab partner?

I did the only sensible thing I could think of: escape.

I turned my back on Teresa and Casey and fled into the tide of people hurrying to lunch or their next class. I didn't care where I was going—I just had to get away.

I hate her, I hate her, I hate her. She's the most wicked person in the world.

I didn't notice Casey following me until I felt his tug on my arm.

I spun around and snapped, "What?" I didn't mean to take it out on him, but thanks to Teresa, I was in no mood.

Casey gave me this look like I was the biggest witch in the world. "Never mind."

He turned and stalked away, our jackalope tucked securely under his arm.

Great. Another victory for my former best friend. All she had to do was say a few simple words, and once again I reacted just the way she wanted.

It had to stop. At some point you've just got to take a stand.

Item one on my to-do list was make a friend—just one friend—right? I had assumed that would be a girl, but beggars can't be choosers.

Not that Casey Connor is such a bad choice. He seems like a nice guy, and funny, which I appreciate. And despite what Teresa said, I doubt that he's gay. Not that I care—it's not like I'm looking for boyfriend material. I just think it's pathetic how Teresa assumes any guy must be gay if he isn't falling all over himself trying to get a look down her shirt.

Anyway, who cares? I just need a friend—boy, girl, goldfish, whatever. Anything to see me through this school year.

And not that it matters, but just for the record, based on my own scientific observations over the past three days, I would say that Casey Connor does like girls. I just get that feeling. And some girl out there probably likes him. I mean, why not? He's funny, smart, and not bad-looking, for a science nerd.

Not that I should talk. I'm just a nerd nerd—no special talent to balance that out. And I'm no great beauty, although I have had a few offers. Yeah, and look how wonderfully that turned out. Adam Ridgeway is now bouncing me off walls.

Anyway, I did the only smart thing I could do. I got over myself, reversed course, and hurried down the hall in the direction Casey had gone. I knew I probably wouldn't be able to catch him before his next class, but I had to try.

Although what I was going to say when I found him was anybody's guess.

Ten

The bell rang, and other than a few stragglers, the hall was pretty empty. No Casey to be found. I'd have to wait until tomorrow and see if I could do any better at proving I wasn't such a rancid person.

I didn't have the heart or the stomach to go to the cafeteria and deal with that whole crowd again. Besides, I still haven't gotten up the nerve to ask my mom for lunch money yet, so I brought my lunch again today, and how much enthusiasm can you work up over peanut butter and jelly?

Still, I was a little hungry, and I needed to keep up my strength. I ducked into the closest girls' bathroom, picked the least disgusting stall, and helped myself to a few bites of PBJ. I don't know, something about the atmosphere just didn't make it all that appetizing. I tossed the rest of my sandwich in the trash and went in search of something else to do until fourth period.

And that's why I know God is with me. Because when I walked into the library, there he was (Casey, not God) (obviously), working at one of the computers.

My heart beat a little faster, not because Casey is such a specimen (not that he's hideous, but let's not get carried away) but because I knew I was probably going to have to apologize before I got anywhere with him.

So I worked on it all the way over. "*Sorry, it wasn't you. . . . Sorry, I was just mad at Teresa. . . . Sorry, didn't mean to be such a pill. . . . Sorry, I'm a mess.*"

He saved me the trouble by asking in British, "Over our snit, are we?"

I was about to sass back, but decided to keep the goal in mind. "Yeah. Sorry."

"Don't apologize," he answered. "Just switch medications."

That kind of ticked me, but if I'm going to get mad at everything everyone says, I'll never make progress.

"So, what're you going to do with that?" I nodded toward the jackalope on the computer desk beside him.

"Hang him from my ceiling," he said in his normal voice. "Here, look at this."

I took that as an invitation to pull up a chair and read over his shoulder.

On the screen was Ms. Shepherd's blog entry from yesterday.

Stayed up until 3:30 reading latest findings on hobbits, a.k.a. *Homo floresiensis,* a.k.a. Flores Woman and the boys. Another bone—jaw this time—12,000 years old. Tolkien had it right, of course, as we always knew, although so far no evidence of hairy feet. Of course, this does nothing to discourage my fantasies about Aragorn.

"Who's Flores Woman?" I asked.

"You know, those skeletons they discovered a few years ago—those three-foot-tall prehistoric people they're calling hobbits."

This time I got it. I was on to Ms. Shepherd. "Oh, right—like jackalopes."

"Uh . . . not quite."

"So they're what—like half human, half rabbit? Although shouldn't that be 'hubbit'?"

"What are you talking about?"

I was so happy to be in on the joke this time. "And who's Aragorn supposed to be—the guy who discovered them?"

Casey gave me the oddest look.

"What?" I asked.

"You are kidding, right?"

I felt a little blip in my confidence, but my mouth kept going. "Oh, what," I said sarcastically, "is this some famous scientific thing everybody knows about but me?"

Casey spoke to me very carefully, like I was a mental patient holding a gun. "Mena, please tell me you're kidding. You do realize that's *Lord of the Rings*."

Oh. One of those. One of those pop culture references I know nothing about because my mind has been kept so blessedly clean all these years.

Usually I'm better at covering for myself. This time it took me by surprise.

I laughed unconvincingly. "Yeah. I know that."

"So you've read it."

"Um, no."

"But you have seen the movies."

I sort of winced and shook my head. I need to learn to lie.

Casey closed his eyes and pinched his fingers against them, like he had a terrible migraine. "Okay, you realize I'm going to have to do an intervention."

"No, that's okay—"

"Okay!" he shouted. All across the library, heads turned. Casey lowered his voice and stared at me intensely. "It is not *okay*, Mena. It is definitely not okay."

This was a new side of him I hadn't seen yet. I kind of enjoyed watching him get so worked up. "What's the big deal?"

"The big deal is that you—a living, breathing member of the human race—have for whatever reason chosen not to avail yourself of the single greatest literary and cinematic achievement of all time. *That* is the big deal. But I'm sure you have a good excuse—just came out of a coma, just regained your sight—something."

I suppressed my smile. "Maybe I didn't feel like it."

"Didn't fee—" Casey gripped the edges of the computer table. "You did *not* just say that."

He inhaled deeply and blew it out slowly, like one of those cleansing breaths Missy taught us in yoga. "All right," he murmured to himself, "it's all right. We can fix this."

Have I mentioned that he is kind of cute in a non-classic, nerdy sort of way?

"Luckily for you," he said, "I have the entire set of extended-version DVDs—with appendices—and if we start right away, you may be cured by next week. Thank God I caught it in time."

Unfortunately, that's when the joking ended. Because for me, this was a time when I'd either have to tell him the truth—or at least some variation of it—or blow him off with some lie I couldn't even begin to think up.

I'd let the whole thing go too far.

Because the truth, of course, sounds ridiculous if you're on the outside. I know from the few times I let things slip that regular people—non-church people—can't believe how many restrictions there are on all of us to keep our minds and hearts pure. No magazines (unless they're Christian); no movies above PG (and even then maybe not, if one of the Christian watch lists says it's dirty); no TV shows featuring sex, drugs, cursing, abortion, adultery, etc., etc. (which my parents have decided is just about all of them); no video games; on and on and on—you name it, we probably can't do it.

The payoff, of course, is that we'll be going to heaven and the rest of the world won't. (Theoretically, although I have trouble with that—why should a good person living out in the jungle, who's never heard of Christ, have to go to hell while some child in Alabama or Nebraska who was baptized but who grows up to do despicable things gets to go to heaven? You see my point.)

But when you're trying to make a friend—just one new friend—and your choice is to reveal all the strange little rituals of your life, knowing he'll give you exactly the same look as when you didn't know who Aragorn was—obviously things aren't as simple as they seem.

I glanced at my watch. "I have to get to class."

"Fine," Casey said. "I'll bring in *Fellowship of the Ring* tomorrow. You can have the whole rest of the week to digest it. I'll bring in *Two Towers* on Monday, *Return of the King* next Wednesday. You'll be cured in no time."

There was no point in letting this go any further. "Look, I can't. But thanks anyway—really." I gathered up my backpack and prepared my escape.

Casey dropped all the dramatics. "Why not?"

I could see he was genuinely perplexed. "Um . . . I just can't. See you tomorrow."

I headed for the door before he could ask me anything else. Some things just defy explanation. It would be like trying to make a fish understand what it's like to play tennis.

Too bad. I mean, it really is too bad. I might have liked hanging out with Casey. But I guess if you have to build a whole friendship on lies and secrets, it's not really going to work.

I'm doomed to be alone.

On the way out of the library I saw Teresa and Bethany and the whole Christian crew coming out of the cafeteria. Wonderful. I would have turned and walked the other way if I didn't have to get to French.

"See you tonight," Teresa told the crowd as they dispersed. She looked over at me to make sure I heard that.

Why does she care so much? Can't she just move on?

Then Teresa added something that made my blood freeze in my veins.

"Shepherd is going down."

Eleven

Tonight at dinner my dad actually looked at me when I asked him a question. And they say there are no miracles anymore.

Of course, it may have been because the question was, "Do you guys mind if I get a little lunch money?"

You'd have thought I asked for my allowance back. As if I'll ever risk doing that.

"You can come work for it," my dad snapped. That one sentence seemed to take an awful lot of effort. He shoveled in another forkful of tuna noodle casserole just to re-fortify himself.

I couldn't believe he even answered. I knew I had to be careful or I'd spoil the mood. "Doing what?"

He addressed his peas and tuna. "Cleaning out the storeroom."

"Okay," I answered without thinking. Believe me, any-thing is better than this banishment. It's bad enough what's been happening on the outside. To face it in my own home has been my own particular hell.

"What do I need to do?"

He answered his casserole. "Clean up the files."

All this time my mother sat there staring at my father, maybe not really believing he had finally decided to talk to me. From the look on her face, I'm not sure she approved. Maybe she had a different time limit in mind—like six months to a year.

"I don't know . . . ," she mumbled to him.

"I'll start on Saturday," I hurried to say before my father could withdraw the offer.

My parents eyed each other. Oh, like this was such a Great Honor, cleaning out all the file boxes they've been accumulating since the last time I helped organize the dungeon of their office storeroom back when I was twelve.

But believe me, I'm willing to do almost anything at this point. And spending a Saturday sorting through papers at my parents' insurance agency is a pretty small price to pay for the hope of family harmony.

Okay, yes—I do feel guilty. I had no idea writing that letter was going to hurt my parents' business. I wasn't thinking about anything back then except trying to right a terrible wrong that had been keeping me up night after night and making me so sick to my stomach I could barely eat anymore.

But I overheard my parents talking the other night about what a disaster this is for their agency. They figure about eighty percent of their customers come from the church. Ever since my parents broke the news that their policies might not include coverage for what Teresa and the other demon children did, a bunch of other people from church have been taking their business elsewhere. And not only are my parents losing that revenue, but now all the people who got sued are threatening to sue my parents for selling them insurance that might not pay off after all.

It's a mess.

But that's not my fault. Why can't anyone see that? It's Teresa's and Adam's and Bethany's and all the other members of the Holy Warriors, or whatever they're calling themselves these days.

And now they're at it again. Are they really going after Ms. Shepherd? For what? She hasn't done anything but be funny and brilliant and clever.

Which is a sin, I guess, to some people.

Please don't let them do anything to her. These people have to be stopped.

Twelve

For a while I thought today was going to be good. Ms. Shepherd sort of made an example out of Adam because he started arguing with her about the jackalope.

"You lied!"

"How did I lie?" she asked him.

"There's no such thing as a jackalope. I looked it up."

"Looked it up where?"

"On the internet."

"Ah," she said, "the internet."

And that led to a whole discussion about whether we should believe everything we read, and how it's destructive to society to trust someone else's observations over our own, and that it's the scientist's duty to always test other people's hypotheses and not fall into lazy thinking.

"But they're not real," Adam kept insisting. "It's just a rabbit with fake horns."

"And at one point people thought the sun revolved around the earth," Ms. Shepherd said. "Question everything."

"So is it real or not?" Lara asked.

Ms. Shepherd answered, "I'll be interested in reading your reports to find out."

Even though she didn't technically tell Adam to his face that he was a lazy thinker, I'm sure he interpreted it that way, because by the time class was over, he obviously needed to take it out on someone, which would be me.

I was so stupid. I wasn't even paying attention as I walked out. One minute I'm stuffing my books into my backpack, and next thing I know I'm bouncing off the nearest wall and my stuff goes flying, and Adam's laughing his head off, and what do I do? Nothing.

I wanted to say, "Do you really think it's cool to beat up girls in the hallway? You really think that makes you a man?" But of course I didn't. Because I, Mena Reece, am a Nice Girl. A weak, pitiful, cowardly girl, but so nice, aren't I?

But even if I did have some biting thing to say, it didn't matter because Adam was already gone.

And then to add to my humiliation, Casey saw all that.

People were streaming through the hall as usual, and Casey helped me retrieve all my papers and books from under their feet and shove them back into my bag. He didn't say a word, for which I am deeply thankful.

When I finally zipped up my backpack, he asked, "Lunch slash library?"

I nodded. I was trying not to cry. It's bad enough to be

as big a chicken as I am—you don't need everyone else to see it.

"We need to start work on our project," Casey said as we made our way through the crowd.

My face was still hot. I was glad for the distraction. "What project?"

"The one for Ms. Shepherd. I think you're going to like it. But we don't have much time—we'll have to get started this afternoon."

"This afternoon? I can't. And what do you mean, we don't have much time? She hasn't even told us what we're supposed to do yet."

"My sister had her for biology, remember? I already know what we have to do. It's all under control."

"Casey, I don't even . . ." Don't what? What was I supposed to say? *Don't know what just happened, don't know you, don't know what's going on, don't know my own name right now?*

"Look," I said, "I can't. I can't go anywhere after school."

"Why not?"

We were just entering the library, so we lowered our voices.

"I have . . . things to do. For my parents." Lame, but I couldn't think of anything else.

"Come on, Mena, it's schoolwork—I'm sure they'll understand. Besides, we only have about two weeks left, then they'll be gone."

"Who?"

"Our test subjects," Casey answered. "Come on—you'll like this. I promise."

He plopped his backpack onto the floor beneath one of the computers, sat down, and logged on.

"Sociobiology," he whispered. "Personality tests. Nature versus nurture. It'll be great."

I was running out of arguments to make, especially since I had no idea what he was talking about.

"Can't we work on it here?" I tried. "During lunch?"

"Negative. Test subjects can't leave my house."

"What are they?"

"You'll see. I only live a few blocks from here. We'll go there after school."

This was getting seriously out of hand. "Casey, I *can't*. There's no point in talking about this. It's impossible."

Casey turned to me, his dark blue eyes gazing directly into mine. It was a little unnerving.

"Mena, I'm going to get you an A plus *plus* this year, but you have to stop fighting me on it. Trust me—this project is going to blow Ms. Shepherd away. Here, look."

He brought up Ms. Shepherd's website and quickly checked her blog for new entries (none) before clicking on the heading *Brilliance*. He scrolled down through the past three years and clicked again.

A document came up on the screen—*Virtual Universes*, by Kayla Connor and Joshua Newman.

"My sister," Casey explained. "She and Josh won their year, so obviously we have to win ours. Ms. Shepherd always posts them. Our names *will* be next."

I was starting to get seriously worried.

"First of all," I said, "there's no way I'll ever be able to come to your house."

"All those rumors about the police finding dismembered bodies in our freezer are completely false," Casey said.

"I'm not joking. I really can't."

"Because?"

"My parents won't let me. I'm like, permanently grounded."

"Well, so I guess the rumors about you are true."

"Why? What have you heard?" I seriously thought he knew something.

"Relax, killer—nothing. Why are you grounded for life?"

"It's a long story."

"I like long stories." He glanced at the clock. "You have twenty-four minutes."

"Forget it. We'll just have to think of another project."

Casey shook his head. "Absolutely not. When brilliance finds you"—he pointed to the school's motto hanging on the wall above the librarian's desk—"you must answer the call. My house, Reece. Today."

"Impossible."

"Not even improbable," he answered. "You don't understand my sister." He switched to British. "Lovely girl, but brutal instincts. Will eat her young if they show the least sign of weakness."

"Casey, I'm really sorry—"

"No need, no need," he said, waving off any further objections. "My man will come round at three o'clock this afternoon. Meet him on the south stairs."

I sighed. Deeply. It's hard to argue with someone who won't take you or himself seriously.

"Look, I'll ask my parents tonight, okay? But I'm not promising anything."

I know there's no way on God's earth that my parents will ever let me go over to a boy's house alone without at least ten other certified Christians around, but I had to come up with something.

"Good," Casey answered, talking like himself again. "But not a day more. We really do have to start right away. These things grow like you wouldn't believe."

"What things?"

Casey smiled mysteriously and pointed at Ms. Shepherd's webpage. "Our future."

This guy is way too much of a brain for me. I think I'm in over my head.

What's going to happen when he finds out I'm so average?

Thirteen

I should have known.

The way that Teresa made a point of making sure I knew about "the meeting" they were having at Bethany's house night before last. That comment about Ms. Shepherd "going down."

The fact that Teresa and Bethany kept looking at me in English this morning and whispering, and Teresa kept laughing.

I should have known from the fact that Pastor Wells had already been talking about "taking a stand," but somehow with all the other mess going on, I'd forgotten. Besides, he's always on the rampage about something.

I especially would have had a clue if I'd looked at Ms. Shepherd's syllabus and seen what she was going to start teaching today.

But it still came as a surprise.

Ms. Shepherd had barely gotten the word "evolution" out of her mouth when suddenly there was this dramatic scraping of chairs. Next thing I knew, almost half of the room—fourteen people, to be exact—stood up, flipped their chairs around, and plopped into their seats with their backs to Ms. Shepherd.

God help us.

Because this was it, the Big Stand, the "taking it to the front lines" Pastor Wells had bragged about.

And you can bet Teresa was loving every ounce of the attention.

I wasn't the only one shocked into silence. You could tell the Back Turners (as I have decided to call them) hadn't warned any of their non-church lab partners ahead of time, so those people were sitting there looking awfully uncomfortable—like maybe they were about to get in trouble, too.

Everyone was as quiet as stones. Casey looked at me with one eyebrow raised. I felt sick to my stomach. *Please, don't do this*, I was praying, but I knew this time it wasn't my fight.

Teresa (who was wearing her *Jesus = Love* T-shirt, the little hypocrite—they were all wearing church shirts of some kind) kept her back to the room while she read a statement:

"We, the students of New Advantage High School, demand that Ms. Antonia Shepherd and all other science faculty cease and desist—"

(Pastor Wells's phrase, I'm sure—he's all about "cease and desist.")

"—from teaching the unproven theory of evolution unless and until they also present the facts associated with intelligent design so that the students of New Advantage

High School may be fully informed of all aspects of this controversy. We, the students of New Advantage High School, demand—"

"I get the picture," Ms. Shepherd interrupted. She didn't sound angry, just matter-of-fact. She quickly surveyed the room, her eyes lighting on Casey. "Mr. Connor, would you come up here?"

He flashed me a little grin.

He went up to the front of the class, and I couldn't help noticing that his olive green shirt looked really good against his pale skin and dark eyebrows and black hair. And for some reason his hair looked particularly good today—all thick and curly, like you could grab huge hand-fuls of it and pull him somewhere.

Not that any of that is important. My point is, it's just weird how your mind wanders when you're under stress.

Ms. Shepherd handed Casey a piece of paper and asked him to read it. Meanwhile, she sat serenely on the edge of her desk and sipped her Starbucks.

I couldn't understand what he was reading at first because it was all legal jargon—*Edwards versus somebody, U.S. Supreme Court number something, blah, blah, blah*—but pretty soon I started to catch on. It was some sort of court ruling about teaching evolution in public schools. Ms. Shepherd had obviously come prepared.

When Casey was done, Ms. Shepherd thanked him and let him sit down before fixing her stern gaze on the rest of us.

"Let's be clear about this," she said. "I teach science.

Intelligent design is not science. It is simply the latest name for a religious philosophy known as creationism. That philosophy says that the universe is too complex to have originated on its own, so some supernatural being must have been involved. That is not something we'll be addressing in this class.

"The United States Supreme Court has made it very clear that teaching creationism in a public school would violate the doctrine of separation of church and state. I happen to believe quite strongly that they are correct. So while I admire your curiosity, Ms. Roberts, you'll have to seek your answers to that particular issue from the clergy rather than from me."

You could tell the Back Turners didn't like that one bit. They chattered among themselves like chimps, not really sure what to do next. I don't think they expected Ms. Shepherd to be so ready for them. Good. Take that.

"As I explained on Monday," Ms. Shepherd continued, "I grade on the basis of test scores, lab work, a special project, and class participation. I do not believe in predestination—whether you receive an F in this class is in your own hands. If you choose not to participate, you understand the consequences.

"Now," she said, her voice brightening, "let us speak of science, shall we?"

I glanced down at my paper. Casey had written, *Love her!*

"We're not finished," Teresa said, still not turning around. It was kind of ridiculous, her arguing to the back of the room.

"You are for now," Ms. Shepherd answered calmly, "or you can leave my class."

Teresa had to think about it. But soon the back of her blond head moved subtly side to side, signaling her cohorts they were staying. How nice for the rest of us.

Ms. Shepherd downed a big gulp of coffee and went right on with her lesson as if nothing had happened. As if she weren't looking at the hind parts of half of her class. As if she hadn't just stuffed Teresa's head back into its hole.

I agree with Casey: *Love her.*

I watched Ms. Shepherd all during the rest of class, and tried to memorize exactly how she used her voice and her gestures and even her eyes to regain control over that room and show everyone that she was not intimidated and would not be treated disrespectfully. I need to be more like that. I shouldn't be so afraid of everyone all the time. Or at least I shouldn't show it.

Casey was grinning all during class like Ms. Shepherd had won some decisive victory. How can I tell him I've been here before, with Pastor Wells taking on a cause, and seen bodies piling up like no one would believe?

These people are not messing around. If they say New Advantage High School isn't teaching evolution anymore, they're going to make sure that happens.

Oh, please. Why did it have to be this year? Why Ms. Shepherd? And why won't my parents let me move to somewhere safe like Alaska or Nova Scotia?

When the bell rang, the murmur of discontent from the Back Turners lasted all the way out into the hall, when

Teresa finally burst out with "That was the biggest mistake of her life."

She glared at me, as if I had something to do with Ms. Shepherd's defiance.

Adam couldn't resist adding his one cent.

"How's it feel?" he asked me, ramming me again with his shoulder. This time I was prepared—I held on to my books. "You like that?" he asked.

He was scaring me, but I gave him as evil a look as I could muster.

"Bet you wish you'd kept your mouth shut," he said.

It took me a moment to figure out what he was talking about.

Then I forced myself to laugh. "You think I want to be sitting there with you guys? Acting like a jerk to Ms. Shepherd?"

Adam smirked. "We're gonna be famous."

That really did make me laugh. Typical Adam. Typical Teresa. Boy, do they love the spotlight.

Before I could find out exactly what he meant by that, I heard Casey ask the question behind me.

"Famous how?"

Adam turned his apelike face toward Casey and stared at him for a second like he was still processing the words. Then he looked back at me. "He your boyfriend?"

My face felt hot. "No."

"He know about you?"

"Shut up." I wasn't sure what he meant by that, but I didn't want to find out. I also didn't know whether to defend myself or to flee. Maybe he was going to say something to Casey once I was gone. Maybe he was going to say something no matter what.

Instead the stupid gorilla decided to ram his shoulder into Casey and bounce him off the wall, too. What a jerk. All meat and muscle and no brains.

I held my breath for a second, wondering what Casey was going to do. Out of the corner of my eye I saw Ms. Shepherd lurking in her doorway. Apparently she wanted to know, too.

Did Casey push back? Shout an insult? Resort to some childish behavior just like Adam would have?

No. Because Casey isn't like other guys. I'm beginning to see that.

And it's not because he was scared, either. Well, maybe he was, but he certainly didn't show it.

He regarded Adam with a look of mild amusement. "Vex not thy spirit at the course of things, for they heed not thy vexation."

"What?" Adam had this look like he wasn't sure what language Casey had just spoken.

I was pretty impressed with Casey myself. I'd never thought of handling Adam like that. I've always leaned toward "shut up."

Adam called Casey a male body part, then stalked off. What a good Christian boy.

For a moment I thought maybe Casey was one of us after all. "Was that from the Bible?"

"Hardly," he scoffed. "Marcus Aurelius."

"Oh." I wasn't sure if I was relieved or disappointed.

"Very good, Mr. Connor."

Casey's head snapped toward the doorway, but Ms. Shepherd had already faded back inside. Casey's pale cheeks burned red.

He turned back to me and cleared his throat. "So, close friend of yours?"

"No."

"He seems to think he knows you."

"Yeah, well, he doesn't." Not as well as he tried, anyway.

Out of habit we started for the library. "So," Casey said, "this should be fun, huh? The Christians versus the lions. A real battle with the wargs. Oh, sorry—more *Lord of the Rings*. Don't worry, we'll fix you right up—I brought *Fellowship* with me. You can watch it this weekend—what am I saying? You're *required* to watch it this weekend. After we work on the project."

"Oh. That."

"Your parents said yes, right?"

"Um, they got home too late," I lied. "I haven't had a chance to ask them yet."

Casey looked at me sternly. "Mena, this is serious. We have to get started. We don't have much time."

"Can you at least tell me what it is?"

"I can, but I won't." He pulled a cell phone out of his backpack. "Dial away."

I bit my lower lip and shook my head.

"What is the problem?"

"I promise I'll ask them tonight." Another lie, but what could I do?

"You promise."

"Yes."

"On pain of death."

"Yes."

"I'll forgive you on one condition." He pulled a thick DVD box out of his backpack. "You must watch this in its entirety—appendices and all—by Monday morning. You may take time off only for homework—most particularly, our project. Otherwise, you will be in front of the TV until your eyes bleed. I'm sorry, but it must be done."

I'm sure I looked less than convinced.

"Swear it."

"I'm not going to swear." But I took the DVD from him anyway, just to shut him up.

But of course I can't watch it. I didn't even bring it home tonight—I had to leave it in my locker. I can't afford to have my parents finding that on me anywhere.

So there you have it, Monday through Friday, first week of school. I can say without a doubt this has been one of the least enjoyable weeks of my life. Not at all the way I imagined it when I used to dream about high school.

And if not for Casey, I'm sure it would have been far worse.

Of course, when he finds out on Monday I've been lying to him, that's the end of that.

Guess I should have enjoyed it more while it lasted.

Fourteen

I didn't even bother writing yesterday. What was there to say? A whole day working in my parents' storeroom, sorting out boxes upon boxes of insurance documents. What more fulfilling work can a girl find?

And now we're here at Sunday. Already. Lately it's been my least favorite day of the week, but considering how the rest of this week has gone, I guess I can't say that anymore.

So here's how it's been going ever since I got kicked out of church: My parents get up early. They do not wake me. They do not want to see me.

I already have my orders: While they are at church until noon, I am to watch a minimum of three religious programs, pray with the TV preachers, and then write a report about what each of the sermons was on.

And then here's the really stupid part: My mother will come home and log on to one of the church websites that list what all of today's TV sermons were about, and she will check my work.

Okay, look. Obviously if she can do that, I CAN DO THAT. Duh.

I tried—I actually did. That first Sunday, I was feeling so bad about everything that had happened, I actually did what my parents wanted me to. I watched three separate programs, listened to loads of special guests and testimonials and "Praise Jesus"es and everything. I even—this is so stupid, because it's so fake—prayed right along with the TV prayers.

But even if you're half brain-dead, you can't help but notice something awfully fishy.

It's all about money. Truly.

"Pledge a thousand dollars today. Call right now. Show God you have faith in Him."

We're supposed to dial up the 800 number, give them our credit cards, send money to the TV people as proof of our love of God and our trust in Him. I don't think so.

They have all these testimonials on the screen, like they're from actual letters:

I pledged a thousand dollars, and the next week my husband got a ten-thousand-dollar raise.

We couldn't afford it, but I said, "Honey, we can't NOT afford it." We called in our pledge, and the very next day we received a check for two thousand dollars.

On and on.

And with actual people's names, like Fred Burstal from Washington Oaks and Margaret Hasher from Pinedale, but what's to stop the TV guys from just making up those names and writing the letters themselves? It's not like there are any forensics people up there on-screen examining the letters and saying, "Yep, this is authentic."

So excuse me for losing a little faith. I'm used to the pitch by Pastor Wells about our duty to tithe ten percent of everything we get, and how our contribution to the church is a showing to God of our gratitude for all He has given us, but Pastor Wells never talks in thousand-dollar increments. I have to give him credit for that.

That first Sunday I wrote up my report, my mom checked it, no praise, no thank you, just silent acceptance. Whatever.

So the next Sunday and the one after that I just did what she did and got the information off the web.

And I'll do the same today, when I get to it. I'm sorry, people, but I have real homework to do. I have hundreds of pages to read for English and world civ, and five paragraphs to write in French, and a few hundred numbers to figure out in algebra. The only class I don't have homework for is biology. Thank you, Ms. Shepherd.

Which reminds me. I'm supposed to be watching *Fellowship of the Ring* right now. Casey said it's about three hours long. Perfect. I could have started watching the minute my parents left for church. But I couldn't lie to them like that.

Sure, technically I'm lying to my parents right now by not watching those TV shows and making up my report, but I am not a dishonest person. And when Casey asks me tomorrow what I thought of it, I'll just have to tell him the truth.

Too bad. You can't please everyone. Lately I can't please anyone.

Fifteen

New week. And I've decided it's time for a new attitude. Time to stop being such a wimp.

So I got to school early today. It's about fifteen minutes before the bell right now, and I'm sitting on the wall outside one of the chemistry classrooms just writing in my fuzzy notebook. I'm not going to bother anyone today, and I'm not going to let them bother me.

I'm going to tell Casey straight out that I didn't watch his DVD, and that I won't ever be able to. My parents have forbidden it, and I respect their decision.

(Which isn't exactly true—the part about respecting their decision. From what I've heard other kids say, I think some of the stuff my parents won't let me watch is probably pretty mild. Not every popular TV show has sex and violence and four-letter words. But it's not really worth the hassle to argue with them about it. I've always had plenty of other things to do, like read and hang out with my friends.

At least I can still read.)

Anyway. I have also decided I am not going to pay attention to Teresa and Bethany or anyone else looking at me and whispering anymore. I'm sick of being paranoid. And if they really are talking about me, then let them. I can't do anything to stop it.

What did Casey say? "Vex not thy spirit at the course of things." I will vex it not.

I've also decided to stop wearing black all the time. It obviously didn't help—people were still able to spot me in a crowd. Besides, dressing like I want to be invisible only makes me feel weak. I have to be strong. So if that means wearing cute boots and nice pants and a sweet blue shirt that looks especially good on me today for some reason if I do say so myself, then so be it.

I will not hide from these people. This is my life. I live in this town, I go to this school, I have as much right as anyone to stand up straight and speak up in class and go into the cafeteria to eat my lunch if I want to (now that I have lunch money from working in my parents' storeroom). I am sick of being so scared.

There's the bell.

Good luck to me.

Sixteen

I'm beginning to see what Charles Dickens meant about it being the best of times and the worst of times. Because there were moments today that sort of balanced out the crud of last week.

First of all, in Mr. Kuhlman's class this morning I was ON. I decided yesterday that instead of just reading the assigned pages in *A Tale of Two Cities*, I should keep on going to the end. So worth it. What I wouldn't give to meet people like that—noble, brave, self-sacrificing. And romantic? Oh yeah. You think anyone would ever go to the scaffold for me?

I even admire Madame Defarge, even though she turned out to be so evil. At least she was strong. At least she stood up for herself. She waited years and years to exact her revenge, and when her time came, she went for it with everything she had.

So I got to raise my hand a lot in Mr. Kuhlman's class, and I even powered through Teresa's snide, mocking looks and whatever mean things she was mumbling under her breath. Who cares. As that banker guy Mr. Lorry says to Lucy at the beginning of the novel to keep her climbing the stairs even though she's so afraid, "Courage! Business!" That's me now. Just keep going.

Then yoga was lovely. Missy must have had a good weekend, because she was extra mellow—which is really saying a lot, since normally I almost fall asleep at the sound of her soft, singy voice. She had us doing gentle stretches for about half an hour, then the rest of the period we just lay on our backs while she guided us through some imagery, and by the end I had to be careful not to snore. It was the most relaxing class I've ever been in in my life.

And then biology.

I don't know where Ms. Shepherd came from or why on earth she's decided to hide out at my particular high school, but all I can tell you is I'm grateful. And I'm also with Casey on this one: *Love her.* You never know what she's going to do next.

Which was just why she did it.

Before class started she was acting all casual, flipping through some science journal, sipping from the Starbucks the giant had just brought her. Instead of leaving this time, the giant hung around, but I didn't really think much of it.

The bell rang. And instantly Ms. Shepherd sprang to her feet and shouted at the giant, "Marry me! Where's your duck? Who stole my spoon?"

Then she pitched her science journal past the giant against the wall, where it hit so hard the pages flew apart.

The giant just stood there expressionless.

Suddenly Ms. Shepherd smiled and said in the sweetest voice, "I'm sorry. I hate you. Let's go to the merry-go-round. Bye-bye now!" Then she took the giant gently by the arm and escorted him to the door.

While we all sat there in freaked-out silence.

Letting go of the giant's arm, Ms. Shepherd turned back to us. "THAT, my friends, is science. That is the unpredictable beauty of our universe. History is unpredictable, human behavior is unpredictable, and subatomic particles? Unpredictable. It's what quantum physics calls the 'uncertainty principle.' It means we cannot—no matter how desperately we try—we CANNOT know with one hundred percent certainty exactly what will happen next. Right? Evolution!"

She caught the Back Turners completely by surprise. When they realized what she had just said, they had to scramble, scooting their chairs around, plopping back into them, trying to act all righteous and dignified about it. It was pretty hilarious, but Ms. Shepherd kept a straight face.

"Perhaps that was predictable," she said, "but not necessarily. Human minds can change."

She thanked the giant and gave him a tip (or maybe she was just paying him for the coffee, but he certainly deserved a tip for standing there and taking that), then got down to today's lesson.

Courage! Business!

"Genius," Casey whispered to me.

Genius and fun, and Casey's right—I love her. I can't

believe how lucky I am to have her this semester. I can only think God has a reason for it. Maybe this is His way of thanking me for what I did with Denny.

I looked over at the Back Turners and almost felt sorry for them. Almost. I mean, obviously they're doing this to themselves. But Ms. Shepherd went on with her lesson, and I could see that most of the kids—including Teresa—wished they could have been watching. It's like sitting with your back to the TV and trying to figure out all the action based on the sound track.

Coffee must be very, very good for Ms. Shepherd's system, because she was all animated today. She spent the hour talking over examples from history and science and life to prove to us that even though we might guess what will happen in the next moment or the next century, we can't absolutely know.

"And this," she said toward the end, "is why evolution rules the day. Because nothing is static. Everything changes. That is the BEAUTY of life. And the successful organisms—the ones like you and me and viruses and sharks and everything else that's out there today—we owe our existence to the genes that kept mutating and adapting all along. THANK YOU, MUTATIONS."

I love it when she says things like that. Like she doesn't even care how weird it sounds.

"If you think about it," she went on, "not a single one of us is exactly like anything that came before. In a way we're all truly freaks of nature. That's what it takes to survive—the freaks shall inherit the earth. Look how well viruses are doing. They mutate and adapt constantly—it's why we have to develop new vaccines all the time to keep killing them.

"Which raises an interesting question," Ms. Shepherd said, glancing over at the Back Turners. "Because if you don't believe in evolution, then you must not believe that diseases change over time. In which case, there would be no need for anyone to get new flu shots every year, because obviously if we've been vaccinated once, that should last forever, right?"

"Brilliant," Casey whispered.

"Just something to think about," Ms. Shepherd said. And then the bell rang.

And I just sat there. I didn't want to move. I wanted to sit there and understand everything I'd just heard.

Because I think until that moment, I was only sort of paying attention. I was treating biology like any other one of my classes—just something to learn so I could get a good grade and move on. I appreciated that Ms. Shepherd was making it fun and interesting, but it was still just a class.

But as of today, I have to admit it: I have a crush on science.

Can you love a thought? Can you love a concept?

Not to be too dramatic, but when Ms. Shepherd explained that about the flu shot and about us all being freaks of nature, it was like something reached inside my chest and yanked on my soul. Like somebody opened up my head and shouted down into my brain, "Do you get it? Mena, are you listening?"

It's just that it all makes sense. In the same way that God makes sense to me sometimes and I really think I can feel Him. I can see the order to things, His purpose behind them. I wish I felt that way more often—about God, I mean—but whenever I do, it's like someone has pumped up my heart with helium, and I can barely keep from floating off into space.

I was still sitting there, all dreamy, when Casey said, "Library?"

"Uh-huh." Somehow I gathered up my books and followed him into the hall.

Teresa and the others had already faded into the crowd. Another blessing. I walked along slowly next to Casey, savoring the buzzing in my ears.

"So," Casey said as we coasted along, "what did you think of *Fellowship*? Incredible, no?"

"Huh? Oh, I didn't watch it."

"What?"

"Yeah," I said, still happily ambling along. "Look, the truth is, I'm never going to watch it. My parents won't let me."

"Because?"

And that's what snapped me back to reality.

Seventeen

How much do I really want Casey Connor to know about my life? You want to be able to pick and choose the good parts—the parts that make you look as little like a freak as possible (no matter what Ms. Shepherd says about the freaks inheriting the earth)—and keep all the other ones to yourself.

But on the other hand, how can you make friends with someone if you don't let him in a little? So there I was, Moment of Decision, and Casey was giving me his usual skeptical/inquisitive/semi-amused sort of look, and it just came out.

"Sorcery."

"Sorcery," he repeated.

"Yes."

He squinted at me and waited for further developments.

"*Lord of the Rings* has wizards, right?"

"Yes," Casey said. "That it does."

"Well, my parents don't approve of stories about magic and sorcery and stuff."

"Because . . ."

I took a deep breath. Here it was, the line I was crossing over, and Casey would either laugh in my face or—or I didn't know what.

"Because sorcery is from the devil."

"Of course," Casey said, without a hint of sarcasm.

Emboldened, I said, "And we don't glorify the devil in our household."

"Unlike the way we do in mine. Midnight sacrifices and bloodshakes and all that."

"I'm serious." I glanced at Margo Alden going by. She'd know exactly what I was talking about. Her mother once confiscated *The Littlest Witch* from Margo's backpack and made the school librarian remove it from the shelves.

"So let me guess," Casey said. "You have also failed to read *Harry Potter*."

I nodded.

Casey collapsed against the nearest wall like he'd been shot. "Must . . . get . . . help. . . ."

He didn't care that people were staring, but I certainly did. That's all I need is to draw more attention to myself. "Thanks a lot." I set off in a huff.

Casey blocked my way. "Come on, Mena, you can't be serious. You actually buy all that?"

"Buy what? That my parents would kill me if they caught me watching any of those movies or reading *Harry Potter*?"

"No, that whole devil and sorcery stuff. Come on—

we actually live in modern times. Telephones, cable, penicillin—"

"Forget it," I said, but I noticed I kept walking with him. I probably should have just said goodbye and let him go on his way. He's never going to understand.

"There's nothing satanic about *Lord of the Rings*, or *Harry Potter*, for that matter. Good triumphs over evil—what's more American than that?"

"Fine," I said. "Enjoy them."

"What if I let you watch it at my house?"

We stopped just outside the library doors. "First of all, there's no way my parents will ever let me go to your house—"

"Have you asked them?"

"No. And second, I would never do something behind their backs like that—"

"Oh, so you've never lied to your parents?"

"No. I happen to prefer the truth."

"So this thing," Casey said, waving his hand, "this thing you're grounded for life for—what's that all about, Little Miss Can-Do-No-Wrong?"

Considering how little respect he had shown for the whole anti-sorcery thing, there's no way I was telling him the other stuff. "None of your business."

"None of my business because it's so terrible I'll be shocked you could do such a thing? Or none of my business because it's another one of these bizarre no-wizards-for-Mena kinds of things? Wait, let me guess—does it involve elves?"

"Shut up."

"Very persuasive," Casey said. He gave me a little bow and opened the door for me.

And that's what's so irritating about him. One minute he's all over me, making me feel like an idiot, and the next he's being all gentlemanly and nice, helping me scrape my books off the floor or holding doors for me or whatever. He'd probably laugh in my face if I told him about the whole Denny Pierce thing, and then buy me a bouquet of roses.

"Can we please just drop this?" I whispered as we entered.

"Of course. Provided you show up at my house this afternoon so we can both get our A's. And I can get my name on Ms. Shepherd's website."

"Forget it. I can't."

"Have you even asked your parents?"

"There's no point."

Casey pulled out his cell phone. "Try."

I swear, that guy is so annoying. "I can't call from in here."

"Then let's go outside."

"You're really a pig."

"Thank you kindly. Now let's go."

Out we went again, into the hall. "I have my own phone, thank you." I punched in my parents' office number. It was all so pointless.

"Mom?" My voice cracked a little. I hadn't really prepared myself. "Um . . . hi."

"What is it, Mena. I'm on the other line."

"Great. Um, I have this project due in . . . in biology? And my lab partner—you know, Casey?—wants me to work on it after school."

"Fine."

"Fine?"

Casey gave me an "I told you so" smirk. As if I needed that.

"Okay," I told my mom, not believing my good luck. "Thanks."

"How will you get home?"

"Um, Casey, can your mom drive me home?"

He nodded.

"Casey's mom will take me."

"Fine," my mother said. "Have her come in when she drops you off." I could tell she was trying to rush me off the phone.

"Casey's mom?"

"No, Casey. Be home for dinner. Bye." And she hung up.

And I had to stand there for a moment, the phone still at my ear, processing what she said.

Have her come in when she drops you off.

Casey's mom?

No, Casey.

Oh. No.

Hadn't I said Casey was a boy? Hadn't I called him a he? Maybe I didn't. Maybe I'd never said it once.

Let me be clear: I know my parents' feelings on this. They are beyond freaked over the idea that someday I might meet some boy who isn't a good Christian, and I'll be drugged or just swept away by hormones, and I'll go back to his place and have sex (they don't even deal with the unprotected part—it's the sex that horrifies them), and then I'll be ruined for my eventual husband, who'll expect me to be a virgin on our wedding night.

I know this because they've only lectured me about a million times. As has Pastor Wells. As has the youth minister. Everyone in my youth group understands what's required here, even though Adam Ridgeway spent a good deal of effort one night trying to convince me otherwise.

So that's why I knew I should call my mom back right away and confess. I couldn't let her believe something false. In fact, not telling her the truth was the same as lying.

But it's not like anything bad was going to happen. Casey's just a friend—not even that—he's just my lab partner.

"So she said okay?" Casey asked.

I nodded slowly. "She said okay."

Eighteen

Casey's neighborhood isn't like mine. Mine is all new and two-story and cookie-cutter, and the only way you know it's your house is by the number and any lawn or porch art you feel like putting out there. We have a black wrought-iron bench to the left of our door. Whoo-hoo.

But the houses in Casey's neighborhood look like ones you see on old reruns—single-story brick, with old, huge trees everywhere. Some of the lawns are pretty ratty, and there are bikes lying on their sides where kids left them, and basketball hoops in driveways, and all these personal, homey touches you'd never get away with in my subdivision. If you had a car with a flat tire out front or an even slightly brown lawn, forget it—the home owners association people would be all over you.

The front of Casey's house is nothing great—just a gravel driveway and a few planters with some flowers—but inside. Inside.

I don't know if I've ever seen a more beautiful home. And I've been in some really expensive places—like Bethany's house—but those are pretty in a manufactured way. All the furniture is new and you can tell it cost a lot, and everything matches and the cushions are placed just so—the kind of house where you're afraid to sit on anything because you might wrinkle it or leave a butt mark.

But walking into Casey's house was like walking into a forest. Seriously. The whole place was wood this, plant that. Huge bookcases on almost every wall, filled floor to ceiling with books. Bushy trees growing from pots. Wooden tables and stools, a wood-frame couch, and these low, big-armed chairs with cushions that didn't match but went perfectly together.

I just stood inside the doorway, staring. "Wow. This is really—"

"Yeah, my mom did all of it."

"What, the decorating?"

"Yeah, and she made all the furniture. *All* of it. Even the lamps and that bowl over there."

"Wow, is that like her job?"

"Nah, just a hobby. She's really an architect."

It didn't seem cool to say, but the most I've ever made for our house is a macramé plant hanger. Oh, and a pot holder. I can't imagine putting together a whole couch from scratch.

"Come meet your test subjects." Casey led me through the kitchen. It had dark wood cabinets, a pale wood floor, a big rag rug, fruit and bread and spices and a coffeepot on the counter—a kitchen that looked like people actually ate there, as opposed to ours, which is all white and glass and stainless steel and perfectly clean and perfectly cold.

"Out here." Casey opened a door at the side of the kitchen, and we stepped into the darkened garage. He flicked on the light, and there they were.

Let me just say, I understand my mother's position. She likes a clean house. She likes order. I gave up long ago trying to talk her into having a pet. "Muddy footprints," she'd say, or "Mena, think of the hair everywhere!"

But looking at those twelve sweet little black faces, and the twenty-four paws propped on the edge of the playpen, and the tails wagging like crazy, and the little barks calling, "Pick me! Pick me!" it was hard to justify not bringing every single one of them home.

"Oh my gosh, Casey."

"I know."

"How old are they?"

"Six weeks. Don't you love them?"

And he was exactly right.

I don't think I realized until that moment what it was really like to be in love. I actually had to press my hand against my heart to keep it from leaping right out of my chest. "Can I hold one?"

"Sure."

I picked up the puppy right at the center of the bunch.

"That one's Christmas," Casey said. "She's a sweetheart."

"Christmas?"

"Yeah, see how they all have different-colored ribbons around their necks? That's to tell them apart. We call them by their colors until someone buys them and gives them a real name. We ran out of regular, so we had to use leftover Christmas ribbon for her."

"Christmas." I snuggled her against my chest. She yawned and licked my chin. I almost started crying. That was it—completely, madly in love.

"How many have you sold?" I asked.

"Four. One of the girls—Lily over there—and three of the boys. You want one?"

Sure, break my heart, why don't you? "I can't. My parents won't let me."

"Too bad. They're going to be great dogs. Abbey's last litter turned out two search-and-rescue dogs and three handicap companions. You can already tell these ones'll be just as smart. Which is why I propose them as our science project. Come on—want to take them out?"

Two by two—one in each arm—we carried a dozen black Lab puppies out of the garage into Casey's grassy backyard, where the puppies immediately began to roll around and run and tumble over each other and experiment with their sharp little puppy teeth on each other's tails and floppy ears.

I was so mesmerized, I didn't see Casey's mom come out.

"Honey, did you offer your friend a snack?" she asked.

"Not yet." And he introduced us.

She was a taller, prettier version of Casey, with that same ivory skin and dark curly hair piled in a scrunchy on top of her head. She had dark blue eyes just like Casey's, too.

And looked about a million years younger than my mom. She wore jeans with black slides and an oversized denim workshirt. And no makeup. My mother would die before she let anyone see her like that.

Mrs. Connor extended her hand. "Nice to finally meet you, Mena. C's told us a lot about you."

"C?"

Casey said, "I'm C, Kayla's K. Otherwise you have to wait until the second syllable to know who's being yelled at."

"That's right," his mother said. "I'm always yelling. You kids hungry?"

I nodded, but mostly I was still puzzling over the whole "C's told us a lot about you." Like what? He's only known me a week. I sure haven't gotten around to mentioning him to my parents. Not that that's a huge surprise. They'd probably schedule a parent-teacher with Ms. Shepherd and demand she assign me to a girl.

"I'll watch the babies," Mrs. Connor told Casey. "I need a break anyway. There might still be some lasagna in the fridge."

I wasn't anxious to let go of Christmas, but lasagna did sound awfully good. Another lunch period in the library had left me semi-starved.

We went through the sliding glass doors back into the living room. "There's some pizza, too," Mrs. Connor called after us.

"I love your house," I told Casey, and I wasn't entirely talking about the place. I loved that there was pizza and lasagna. I loved that the whole house smelled like wood and books and felt like a place you could really relax.

I loved that Casey's mom actually talked like a real person to us instead of the fake way my mother talks to my friends—"And how was school? And how are your parents? Be sure to tell them I said hi." Like anyone actually tells someone hi.

I followed Casey to the kitchen. "Your mom's really pretty."

"Thanks." He seemed sort of embarrassed by the compliment. He opened the fridge and pulled out a casserole dish.

"Is it all right if I look around?" I asked.

"Help yourself. Don't try to take anything—we have hidden cameras."

While Casey warmed up lasagna in the microwave, I wandered back into the living room. Okay, I admit it—to snoop. You can tell a lot about somebody by the little things they leave around.

Like the pictures on the mantel. There were a bunch with Casey at various ages and a girl I assumed was his sister. They looked almost identical, except she was a little taller. There were a few pictures with Mrs. Connor and a guy I assumed was their father. Obviously Casey and his sister got their hair from their mother, since their dad's was this thin, wispy reddish blond.

"He died," Casey said matter-of-factly. I turned to find him carrying in our plates.

"Who?"

"My father. It was really sad. You want some milk?"

"Oh, I—"

"I'll be right back." Casey disappeared into the kitchen before I could think of something better to say.

But you have to say something, right? So when he came back I went with the usual, "I'm really sorry."

"It wasn't your fault." He handed me my milk. "Want anything else?"

"No, but—"

"So, the project," Casey interrupted, sinking onto the couch.

Okay, so obviously he didn't want to talk about it. I can take a hint. I stopped trying to console him and sat on one of the cushy chairs.

"We only have the litter for about two more weeks," Casey said, "so we need to get on this right away. If you agree." He shoveled in a forkful of lasagna.

"Why only two weeks?"

Casey mumbled past his food. "Owners like to take them at eight weeks."

Already I was missing my little Christmas.

Casey gulped down some milk and went on. "So I thought we'd start today, making a chart with all of their relevant information—height, weight, personality score—"

"What's that?"

Casey waited until he'd swallowed another massive bite. By the way, his mother does make killer lasagna. We were eating it like a pack of wild dogs.

"It's this test to see how bold they are, which of them like being handled, which don't—that sort of thing. I have some things to add to it, of course. For instance, I've noticed Lily is a real music lover, whereas Red would rather hear two pans banging together. I thought we'd start with a baseline today, then observe any changes over the next two weeks. It should be fascinating. So what do you think? Game?"

I nodded and chewed. "So you really think Ms. Shepherd will like this?"

"Definitely. She's more of a cat person, but I think she'll appreciate the spirit of what we're doing. You know, the whole evolution thing."

I confess I didn't really get what he meant. Casey must have seen that on my face.

"You know," he clarified, "the sociobiological aspects of pack living, the whole natural selection and breeding for advantage—that sort of thing."

"Uh-huh." I didn't really understand, but I was sure Casey had it all figured out.

"Ms. Shepherd's going to love it," he continued. "You saw with our potato analysis how much she appreciates people going off the grid. That's why my sister's project won. She and Josh were really out there. Oh, look, here's Abbey."

A large black Lab came shuffling into the living room, her feet dragging, head hanging low.

"Poor girl," Casey said. "She's so exhausted. Those pups are on her night and day. Come here, Ab." The dog picked up her pace and approached Casey for a nice ear scratch.

"How come she wasn't in the garage with the puppies?"

"We try to give her breaks. She comes in here and sleeps on my bed when she wants to get away."

Abbey glanced outside to where her puppies were playing on the grass. She ambled over to the sliding glass door and waited patiently.

"Sure you want to go out, girl?" Casey set his plate on the coffee table and went to open the door. "Watch," he told me. "They'll be on her like piranhas."

Sure enough, the minute the door opened, from all over the yard twelve little black heads shot up, and immediately the puppies swarmed toward their mother.

"Poor Ab," Casey said. "She's got to be so sore."

She trotted ahead of her crew for a while, puppies yipping excitedly behind her. Finally one of them caught up with her, and the jig was up. He clamped on to her hind leg and wouldn't let go.

"That's Bear," Casey said. "Master of the takedown. Although Pink's pretty good at it, too. Look at her—she's such a bruiser."

The stout little puppy with a pink collar had taken hold of the other hind leg.

Abbey gave up on escape and lay on her side in the grass while twelve sets of sharp teeth descended on her. Bear and Pink in particular went at it with gusto.

Casey banged on the glass door. "Hey!" His mother looked up and waved. Casey pointed to the mass of suckling puppies. "Get him off her!" He turned to me. "I swear Bear is going to rip off one of her teats from the roots someday. No finesse." He banged again, but his mother misunderstood and simply smiled and waved again.

"So, your mom works at home?" I asked.

"Yeah. She has an office in back." Casey watched the carnage in the backyard for a few more moments, then sighed and returned to the couch. He promptly polished off the rest of his lasagna. "We'll have to wait a little while now for them to finish eating. They're going to be really sleepy. But at least we can get the weighing and measuring done today and establish a baseline."

"Okay, sure." It sounded like he had it all planned out, which was fine with me. I'd be happy just to record whatever he told me, like I did with the potato thing. I'm better as an assistant scientist anyway.

But it was not to be.

"You should think of whatever experiments you want to do," Casey said. "We have a whole two weeks."

"Like what?"

"I don't know, whatever pack dynamics you think might be interesting. Or individual personality and physiological differences." He shrugged. "Anything you want."

I didn't even know what I wanted. No, that's not true—I did know. I just wanted to hang out at the Connors' house with Casey and the puppies and eat lasagna and pizza and never have to go home again. Was that too much to ask?

Casey picked up his empty plate and headed toward the kitchen. "Want another piece? Or we've got ice cream."

"No thanks." It wasn't at all like hanging out with Teresa. She's always pretending to be on a diet, even though she's as skinny as a pencil. If this is how boys eat all the time, I could get used to hanging out with them.

With Casey out of the room for a minute, I seized the opportunity to sneak over and study the pictures on the mantel again. Now that I knew his father was dead, I wanted a better look.

But before I could do much spying, the front door slammed open and in burst the solution to at least one of my problems, although I didn't know it right away.

"C? Get out here, you little rat! I'm gonna kill you!"

Nineteen

"Hello, sister dear."

"Don't sister dear me, you brat. I hate your living guts. Why didn't you tell me?"

She was huge—six foot at least—and other than that looked exactly like Casey except her curly black hair went all the way to her waist. She wore wire-rimmed glasses, camo pants, black sports sandals (which showed off her bright red toenails), and a black T-shirt that said *United States of Lies*.

And right behind her—I'm not kidding—in walked the giant. The one who brings Ms. Shepherd her Starbucks— that guy. It was surreal.

Casey leaned against the kitchen doorway and continued nonchalantly stuffing his face.

"Start talking," his sister demanded, "or Josh is gonna beat you to a bloody pulp."

Josh the Giant seemed as unimpressed by that news as Casey. "Any more?" he asked, nodding at Casey's plate.

Casey jerked his thumb over his shoulder. The giant ambled past him into the kitchen.

"Lab partner," Casey said, in case I hadn't figured out who Josh was, which I hadn't. Obviously in their year Ms. Shepherd assigned partners by height.

"Want some?" Casey asked his sister.

"Don't change the subject," she snapped.

"Which is?" Casey asked calmly.

"Which is the fact that I have to hear about this from Josh this morning, rather than from you, you maggot-headed ingrate. Why didn't you tell me? Half your class in revolt and you don't tell me? The creationists come to town and you don't think you'd better get me that information right away? What, are we not related anymore? Did I steal your inheritance or something?"

"Be nice," Casey answered, clearly enjoying his sister's outrage.

"Nice?" she shouted. "You're lucky I don't pummel you, you little worm. Start talking. I want names, profiles, affiliations—everything you know and everything you're gonna find out for me, because now you owe me, you traitor. The school board meeting's tonight, and I need to come prepared."

Casey pointed his fork across the room. "Actually, Mena knows them a lot better than I do. Ask her."

NO. I widened my eyes at Casey and shook my head, but it was too late. His giant sister rounded on me.

And she smiled—I swear—this big, friendly smile like the one their mother had given me earlier. And it's like her whole personality changed right before my eyes. If I hadn't been so afraid of her, I would have loved that smile. Instead it was like staring into the teeth of a shark.

"*You're* Mena? The lab partner?" She looked me over. "How entirely excellent." She strode toward me, hand outstretched. I shrank against the fireplace.

"Fear not," Casey told me. "Tranquilizer guns at the ready."

"Ignore the moron," Kayla said cheerfully. "So nice to meet you." She gripped my hand like I was made of metal. "So, you know these lunatics, huh? Unbelievable what society is turning out these days. But they picked the wrong teacher to mess with. I want all the dirt you have. Let's cut 'em off at the legs."

"But I'm not—"

"Go with 'no comment,' " Casey advised. "Then run for the door while I distract her."

Kayla pressed on. "So, they're friends of yours?"

I snorted. "No."

"Okay, enemies?"

I wasn't so quick to answer that time. Kayla guessed the truth.

"Great," she confirmed. "Enemies. So how do you know them?"

"Well, not exactly enemies," I lied. "Just . . . not friends anymore."

Kayla was diplomatic. "Right. No longer friends. And how did you say you know them?" She loomed over me, outwardly friendly but huge. I had no choice but to answer.

"Um . . . from church."

"Which church?"

"Paradise Christian." I glanced at Casey. He gave me an encouraging shrug.

Josh returned to the living room, plate piled high with both lasagna and pizza. He settled onto the couch to watch Kayla and me like we were on TV.

"If you go to the same church," Kayla asked, "why aren't you part of the protest?"

Good question—I had to give her that. "Um, because . . . I sort of got kicked out."

Both Casey and his sister lifted just their left eyebrows, like they'd rehearsed it.

"Interesting," Kayla said, her voice all silky. She draped her arm around my shoulders and gave me a squeeze. "Mena, my love, I think you're my girl."

That semi-freaked me out. "Excuse me?"

"Oh no," Casey objected. "She's here for our project."

"Tough," Kayla answered. "This is more important."

"What is?" I asked. I really had no idea what was going on.

"She wants you to write for the paper," Casey said. "K's the editor."

"Editor in chief," Kayla corrected, "and you don't have to write it, you just have to be my source."

Casey said, "We don't have time—"

"If you had done even your *minimal* duty as a brother," Kayla answered, "by telling me on Friday, when this all went down—or even Saturday or Sunday, you little twit—I might not be so under the gun. As it is, I'm on deadline, and this *has* to make the front page."

"Too bad," Casey said. "We have work to do."

Kayla linked her arm in mine. "Girl talk," she told her brother. "We'll be right back."

"Five minutes!" Casey shouted after her. "I'm timing!"

Kayla dragged me out to the hallway. "Hate to break it to you, friend, but my little brother has a *huge* crush on you."

"What?"

"So ignore anything he says—he's just besotted."

Before I could process any of that—and believe me, I wanted to—Kayla forged on. "Look, Mena, this is huge— HUGE. This is our own Scopes Monkey Trial, right on our doorstep."

"Our what?"

"It's going on all over the country. Republicans and their Christian taskmasters infiltrating school boards one by one, trying to make sure no one ever hears that there was a man called Darwin or there's such a thing as evolution. They're ripping those sections out of science textbooks and firing teachers who dare speak the word. Can you believe it? Morons. Total rubbish."

If it had been Casey, he would have said that last part with a British accent.

"It's their way of infecting the populace and marginalizing dissent. They want to resurrect theocracy. And they're doing it school by school, book by book, child by child, pretending no one's going to notice and no one's going to stop them."

Kayla poked me on the chest. "But not this school, buddy boy. Not on my watch. And you, Mena my friend, are the key to it all."

Her finger felt like an ice pick. "Why me?"

"Because you used to be part of that whole . . . group thug mentality." She smiled. "And now you're not."

"It's not like I left," I reminded her. "They kicked me out."

"All the better. You're my perfect whistle-blower."

"I'm not—"

"Time's up!" Casey yelled from the living room. "Go play with your own friends now."

"So what's it going to be?" Kayla asked me. "You in, you out?"

Before I could answer, she held up her hand. "Wait, I guess I should ask first. You don't agree with what they're doing, do you? The whole chair-turning-around thing?"

"No," I answered truthfully, but I didn't say it was because I thought they were being disrespectful to Ms. Shepherd.

"And you don't agree we should return to the days of Copernicus, when men of science were jailed and even killed for telling the truth?"

"Of course not—"

"And you do realize the earth is billions of years old—not just ten thousand or whatever they're saying Genesis works out to be, right? Because there are fossil records and proof—Ms. Shepherd went over that, right?"

"Yeah, I guess—"

"Okay," said Kayla, satisfied that we were on the same side. "So you'll do it?"

"Do what?"

"Tell me everything. Be my source."

"No, I don't think that would be—"

"Just the background," Kayla said. "I'll take it from there. I just need to know everything you know—who these people are, why they're doing it, who put them up to it, what they're planning next."

"I don't know what they're planning next. I don't know anything."

But as I was saying it, my mind flashed on Pastor Wells. Of course I knew what he was up to. And even though I hadn't been at that meeting at his house last Wednesday night, I could perfectly picture what had happened. I'd been at a meeting just like it back at the start of junior high.

Maybe this was my chance. To do something. To stop them before they could ruin someone else's life. And if it was Ms. Shepherd I could save, then all the better.

But before I got to that and gave Kayla any of the information she might want, there was this other matter, more pressing. It had been in the back of my mind all afternoon. Maybe it was the fact that Kayla was asking me to defy my parents once again—because make no mistake, joining forces with Kayla against Pastor Wells and my old youth group would not bring joy to my parents' hearts—that made me bargain now.

"I need a favor," I said. The idea had been stewing in me since the first time I heard Casey call his sister "K." I'm no genius, but sometimes I do have moments of inspiration.

Kayla straightened back up. Until then I hadn't

noticed she was bent over and right in my face. "Of course. Once you say you're on the team."

"I'm on the team," I answered, my stomach knotting, wondering if this was the last short step to hell. "Within limits."

"No limits," Kayla said. "Now, what's the favor?"

"I need a ride home tonight. And I need you to pretend you're Casey."

Twenty

By the time Kayla was through grilling me (and Casey was through coming into her room every five minutes to complain about it), I had only forty-five minutes to devote to the puppies. But we still managed to weigh and measure them, and I got to smell twelve doses of puppy breath, which has to be one of the sweetest scents on earth.

I wasn't quite sure how the whole Kayla/Casey thing was going to work. My plan was still pretty vague. As I helped Kayla search for her car keys, I started to develop my strategy.

"I'm just going to call you K, all right?"

"I'll try to remember that. Josh?" she shouted toward the living room. "Are you sure you don't have them?"

"Never touched them."

Kayla dumped out her denim purse onto her unmade bed and sifted through the debris. Her whole room was as disorganized as her purse was. Clothes on the floor and draped over furniture, books on every surface, her computer desk piled with printouts and newspapers and

Time magazine and *U.S. News & World Report* and something called *Adbusters*. Not a teen or fashion mag to be found.

She had posters all over the place, telling me to vote and question authority and swish and swallow when I can't brush. ("I like the little tooth guy," Kayla explained. "Kind of reminds me of Josh.")

My mother would never in a hundred million years let me keep my bedroom like that. She'd call in the guys in the decontamination suits.

Casey's room was pretty orderly, but it had its quirks, too. He wasn't kidding about hanging the jackalope from the ceiling. There were all sorts of things hanging from there—a model of the galaxy; three different kinds of *Star Trek* ships; a Nimbus 2000 broom (Casey had to explain that was from *Harry Potter*); and a handmade mobile featuring army men, disembodied Barbie heads, and plastic figures of Yoda and Obi-Wan.

"You know who they are, right?"

I assured him I did. I may not know every piece of pop trivia, but it's not like I live in a cave.

Everything hanging from the ceiling came down so low, I almost felt like I should walk hunched over.

"It's to keep K out," Casey explained. "No head clearance."

I felt kind of bad about some of the name-calling and bickering I'd seen between the two of them earlier. On the other hand, it didn't seem to bother Casey at all. In fact, he had looked amused.

"Do you . . . like your sister?"

"Love her to death. Why?"

"Um . . . before, it was kind of . . . dramatic."

"K likes to get up a good head of steam. Better to just let it play out."

After weighing and measuring the pups out in the garage, we came back to Casey's room and made up our chart.

At one point Casey's hand accidentally brushed against mine, and I jerked away like he'd burned it. Then I felt like an idiot. I almost wish Kayla hadn't said that about him having a crush on me. Now I feel all weird.

Not that I think it's true. I'm sure she just said that because she likes teasing her brother, and so telling me he likes me is just an extension of that. Besides, Casey doesn't act the least bit like he has a crush on me. I think I'd know, wouldn't I? We're just friends. And right now that's all I need.

At six I knew my fun times were over. I had to get home for dinner. So that's when Kayla started her key search and I prepared for the next stage of lying to my parents.

Finally she located her keys under a mound of dirty clothes and we were off.

"It runs," Kayla told me when she saw me eyeing her car skeptically.

The front bumper was crushed, there were cracks in the windshield, and the seat covers looked like they'd been ravaged by cats.

"It was my dad's," Kayla said. "I've kind of let it go."

After letting her pump me for information about the

Back Turners all afternoon, maybe I felt entitled to ask a few questions myself. Or maybe I was just too curious to be polite. "So, how did he die?"

"Cancer," Kayla said, sliding in next to me and strapping down. "Fast, too. It was ugly."

"How long ago?"

"Three years. I was a freshman, C was in sixth." Kayla gave me a moment for that to sink in. "Kind of rough on the little guy."

"I'm really sorry. That must have been awful."

"Yeah, pretty hellish. But if it was going to happen, I'm glad it was that year."

"Why?"

"Ms. Shepherd. She was my biology teacher—C probably told you that. Jeezus!" Kayla dodged a blue minivan at a stop sign and gave the driver a good dose of her horn. "Hang up and drive!" she shouted out the window.

When my nerves had settled down, I said, "So . . . Ms. Shepherd?"

"Right. Saved my life. No question."

"How?"

"Because she was the only person who'd tell me the truth. Everyone else—the doctors, my parents—kept trying to protect me, but at least I could go to Ms. Shepherd and say, 'Okay, now he's peeing blood. Now he's coughing up green chunks—what's that mean?' All the really gruesome stuff. And she'd always give it to me straight. She'd log on to this hospice website and we'd go through the death signs and figure out where he was on the scale."

"That sounds awful."

"Yeah, but which would you rather? My dad was dying—nothing I could do about that. If my parents had their way, I'm sure I never would have known how bad it was until he was on his last breath."

"They probably didn't want you to worry."

"How can you not?" Kayla asked, her voice rising. "Anyone could see how bad he was. Toward the end, in the hospital, he was practically disappearing into his bed, like it was sucking him under." Kayla shook her head. "It's hard to explain. You'd have to see it for yourself. But you definitely know when someone's about to go. I'm just glad Ms. Shepherd was honest enough to tell me so I knew three months ahead of time instead of three days."

"Did Casey know?"

Kayla made a face. "I was as bad as my parents. I didn't want him to worry. How's that for hypocritical?"

"But he was only what, eleven?"

"His dad was going to die whether he was eleven or not. I should have prepared him better." Kayla shrugged. "What're you gonna do?"

We were nearing my subdivision. I pointed to the entrance.

Kayla whistled as she made the turn. "Fancy."

"Not really." The truth was, I liked her neighborhood and her house much, much better.

"So what about you?" Kayla asked. "Both parents still kicking around?"

"Yeah."

"That's good."

Great. Bring on the guilt. On top of everything else, now with Kayla's help I was about to lie to them.

I felt compelled to explain. "Um, this whole pretending to be Casey thing? I just want you to know I don't usually lie to my parents. Almost never. They've just been a little . . . weird lately."

"No sweat," Kayla said. "Pretty harmless, if you ask me. I mean, what's the problem with being at my house anyway? It's not like we're smoking weed or having orgies. And my brother's about as innocent as they come."

Which brought me right back to thinking about her earlier statement.

"How do you . . ." I didn't want to sound too interested, but I still needed to know. "You said Casey . . . likes me?"

"Are you kidding? Poor guy can barely think."

"I don't . . . see that." It felt really weird to be talking to Kayla about this, but I was too curious to stop. "So did he . . . I mean, did he actually say he likes me?"

"God, no. You think he'd ever hand me ammunition like that? But trust me. Usually all he talks about is *Lord of the Rings* and science fiction. Lately it's been 'Mena said this, Mena said that.' Kind of disgusting, if you want to know the truth."

I couldn't think of a single thing I'd ever said in front of Casey that would be worth repeating.

"He thinks you're funny," Kayla said.

"I'm not funny."

"Obviously. He also let slip that you're pretty, which is true."

"Shut up," I mumbled.

"Aww." Kayla reached over and pinched my cheek. "That's so cute!"

I brushed away her hand and tried not to smile.

We were almost at my house. Time was running out.

"Okay, so we'll say you're my lab partner—"

"No go," Kayla said. "Not believable. I'm too old and sophisticated. Let me handle this. Parents love me."

We pulled into the driveway and Kayla jumped out. She leaned back and took in the enormity of our two-story house. "Wow. How big's your family?"

"Just the three of us."

"Huh."

I could tell she didn't approve. But what can I do about it? I didn't pick our house.

I opened the front door and called out, "Mom?"

She poked her head around the wall between the kitchen and dining room and hushed me with her hand. She had the phone to her ear.

"Perfect," I whispered to Kayla. "Just wave and go." In a louder voice I said, "Okay, thanks for the ride, K," and started to maneuver Kayla toward the door.

She ignored me and waved to my mother, then plopped into the nearest chair.

"I'll just wait to say hi," she told me.

"No, really—"

She grinned. "Trust me."

After a few minutes my mom hung up and came out to greet us. Kayla unfolded herself from the chair and straightened to her full height. Which is pretty impressive when you see it at first—I could tell my mother thought so.

"Mrs. Reece? Hi. I'm Kayla Connor. My friends call me KC."

OH. MY. GOSH. She's brilliant. Or I'm just stupid. KC equals Casey. I never even thought of that.

They shook hands. My mother winced a little at Kayla's grasp.

"So nice to meet you," Kayla said. "Your daughter's a real science whiz."

Okay, now that was stretching it, but my mother obviously didn't want to say so in front of company. She flashed me an odd look, since we both knew my science grades in junior high were nothing to sing about.

"So," my mother said, taking in Kayla's height again, "you're in Mena's class?"

"Oh no," Kayla replied with a laugh. "I'm part of the teen mentoring program. We go all over the school—math, science, languages. . . ."

Kayla sort of drifted off with a nod, and we stood there in silence waiting for her to entertain us some more. My mother and I don't really have much to say to each other these days.

Kayla broke the spell with a clap. "So, Mena. I'll see you tomorrow, right?" She punched my arm. "Good work on that graph today."

"Um, thanks . . . for the ride and all."

"No sweat." Kayla shook my mother's hand again, much to my mother's surprise. She's not used to such businesslike behavior from people under twenty. "Nice to meet you, Mrs. Reece. Keep up the good work."

My mother fumbled for an appropriate response, but Kayla was already heading for the door. Her stilt-like legs covered the distance in three strides.

"Remember," Kayla added as she turned the knob, "the x-axis carries the stable elements, the y is the volatile."

"Okay." I had no idea what she was talking about. "Thanks."

Kayla smiled and exited.

"Well," my mother said, "she certainly seems like a mature young woman."

"She is," I agreed.

We stood there another awkward moment, then my mother said, "Go finish your homework. Dinner won't be for a while. Your father has a meeting."

"Want me to set the table?"

"No, do your work."

And the freezing conditions continue.

I waited until dinner was almost over before telling my parents this science project is going to take at least two weeks, and I'll have to go to Casey's house every day.

"She seems like a responsible young lady," my mother reported to my father. "I think she'll be good for Mena. Although we should meet her parents at some point—"

"Mom, she's just my mentor, not my best friend or anything."

"What do we know about this girl?" my father asked. "Do they do any sort of drug testing before they let kids become mentors?"

"Look," I said as calmly as I could, "I'm sure Kay—" I stopped because I almost said her real name, but then I realized it was all right—my mother already knew. I just have to be careful never to say "he."

"I'm sure KC doesn't drink or do drugs," I told my dad. "She's really into school."

"She isn't the druggie type," my mother confirmed.

As if she can tell things about people just by spending five minutes with them. She's known me my whole life, and she doesn't understand who I am at all. I'm sure if I had shown her that letter to Denny before I sent it, she would have tried to talk me out of it. Or just plain forbidden it. She doesn't understand that sometimes you have to tell the truth, no matter what the consequences.

"All right," my father said, "but not on Sundays. You're still on restriction."

"Yes, sir."

Great. So I still have to waste three hours of my life pretending to watch TV preachers, just because I'm not wasting three hours of my life hanging out at church anymore.

Not that it was all a waste. I don't mean that. I'm glad I was brought up knowing about God and the Bible. I feel sorry for kids who weren't. It's just that what does sitting around with Teresa and Adam and the rest of them at church all day, bowling and playing darts and eating fries in the church food court, have to do with being a good Christian? Just because I don't go to church anymore doesn't mean I'm suddenly a bad person or I've forgotten everything I ever learned.

In fact, I think I could learn a lot more than I ever did at church just by sitting down on Sunday mornings and reading the Bible for a while. That sounds a lot better than listening to three hours of TV preaching where all they really want me to do is send them my money so I can be saved. Give me a break.

But if that's what I have to do to earn back my parents' trust, I guess I have to do it.

Of course, lying to them about Casey seems to contradict that, but what else am I supposed to do? He's the only person—well, him and Kayla now—at that entire school who wants anything to do with me. He's a nice guy. He's interesting and fun. And he's going to help me get an A in science just for showing up and playing with his puppies. What could be wrong with that?

So why do I feel so guilty?

Twenty-one

I should have known something was up in English this morning, because Teresa was acting so abnormally bouncy (and I'm not just talking about the *Jesus Loves Me, This I Know* T-shirt she was wearing—two sizes too small as usual). She and Bethany had some serious whispering to do before class, and they looked over at me at least five times.

But I tried to put it out of my mind. I can honestly say those people aren't bugging me as much this week. Maybe it's because I've found someone else to hang out with. Or maybe I'm just getting over them.

Then right before I went into biology I ran into Casey. "This should be interesting," he said as he opened the door.

There at the front of the room stood Kayla and Josh and some guy with a camera. Kayla wore jeans and her sports sandals and a T-shirt that said *President Her.* Ms. Shepherd (wearing wrinkled clothes, as usual) had her Starbucks and Kayla sipped a grande Frappuccino, and they were both laughing and carrying on like old pals.

"Under that smiling exterior," Casey said ominously as we took our seats, "lies the soul of a ruthless killer."

"What's going on?"

"The usual—investigation, confrontation, Kaylafication. No survivors. I recommend writing a will."

"Why? What'd I do?"

"K says that stuff you gave her yesterday was pretty hot. I tried to warn you."

"She just asked me a few questions—"

"Oh, no, no. Where K's concerned, there's no such thing as a simple question. She's like a tick. She finds a little blood and she gorges herself. I doubt she slept at all last night, judging from all the stuff I saw on her website this morning."

"Wait a minute—your sister has a website?"

"Of course. In case you haven't noticed, K has an awful lot of opinions. And for some reason she seems to think everyone in the world would like to hear them." Casey chewed the end of his pen. "To be fair, she does get about eight hundred unique visitors a day—"

"Eight *hundred*? A *day*?"

"Yeah. A lot of other bloggers link to her. And then there are all the orders for Josh's T-shirts."

I'm sure the look on my face was one big "huh?" but the time for chatter was over. There was only about thirty seconds left before the bell, and all around us people were growing restless.

Kayla signaled for her photographer to move toward the back. She and Josh slipped over toward the side. The

Back Turners sat facing front, poised for action. Everyone was in position.

The bell rang, Ms. Shepherd said the magic word, and the Back Turners flipped their chairs, just like it was a musical number they'd been rehearsing for weeks.

Kayla actually laughed out loud. I guess it is pretty funny the first time you see it. Her photographer clicked and flashed.

Everything seemed to be going well, until the door to the classroom opened and there stood our principal, Mrs. Martinez.

Along with her Very Special Guest.

I muttered a very bad word.

"Who's that?" Casey asked me.

"Our pastor."

I slumped down in my chair.

But still he found me, eyes right on me.

Shoot. But that's not what I was thinking.

I could feel the sweat sliming my palms.

I hate that I'm so weak.

If anyone should feel uncomfortable, it should be him, not me. I'm not the one being sued. I'm not the one who set out to ruin some boy's life.

Yet I was the one trying to hide under my desk.

Mrs. Martinez didn't look so good. Her face was all gray and pinched, like she was having stomach problems. I could relate. She motioned for Ms. Shepherd to join her and Pastor Wells out in the hall.

Kayla whistled for her photographer, and the two of

them followed. They were only gone a moment before Mrs. Martinez opened the door and ordered them back inside. Kayla still looked pretty happy. Her photographer must have gotten a few pictures.

She sauntered over to Casey's and my desks and gave my ponytail a tug. "Up till three this morning," she told me, "but I'm telling you, helluva story we've got here. You're gonna love it. We're delaying the issue until Friday so I can add in all the stuff from today. And boy, you shoulda seen the bloodbath at the school board meeting last night—hoo-wee! Wait'll I lay it all out—it'll make your teeth curl. We're talking the first high school Pulitzer."

She reached out and fluffed Casey's hair into an even larger heap of curls. "How's it goin', little bro?"

He flicked off her hand like it was no more bothersome than a mosquito. And he didn't even bother fixing his hair. I kind of liked that. "What'd you find out?" he asked his sister. "In the hall?"

"Big doin's. Wouldn't wanna ruin it for you. Just a little compromise they worked out at the school board last night so we could get outta there before sunrise. So," she asked me, "any flak from your mom?"

"Huh? Oh no—she bought it."

"Great. Listen, I'm gonna be a little tight for time this afternoon. Gotta meet some people for the paper. If you need a ride again, I'll have to take you early."

"Okay, thanks—"

"That's great, K," said Casey, showing some irritation.

"Don't worry about us. I'm sure we'll get to our project one of these days. What, is it the competition that scares you? Can't stand to see our names on Ms. Shepherd's website?"

"Don't get your tighty-whities in a bunch, little man. I'm only talking half an hour. You'll still have plenty of time." Kayla winked at me. "He's so cute when he's freakin' out."

The door opened again, and the trio returned. Ms. Shepherd did not look happy. In fact, the way she was glaring at Pastor Wells, I'm surprised his skin didn't melt right off his face.

"Apparently," Ms. Shepherd said, her lips tight, "this gentleman will be allowed to make a statement."

I hated myself for looking at Teresa right then, but I couldn't help it—it was just a reflex. She flashed me a triumphant smile.

"Unbelievable," Kayla said, making no attempt to lower her voice. Ms. Shepherd gave her a subtle shake of the head. Kayla folded herself into the empty chair beside me and flipped open her pocket-sized notebook.

Pastor Wells held out his hand for the sheet of paper clenched in Ms. Shepherd's fist. "May I?" She didn't look at him as she handed it over. Pastor Wells slipped on his glasses and read. " 'Experts agree—' "

Ms. Shepherd made a choking sound like she had just swallowed glass. She gulped down a big swig of her Starbucks.

Pastor Wells began again. " 'Experts agree that Darwin's so-called theory of evolution is just that—a theory.' "

"Like the theory of gravity?" Kayla called out. "Or don't you believe in that?"

A bunch of us laughed, but Mrs. Martinez was not amused. "Miss Connor, that will be enough."

"Here for the paper," Kayla answered, waving her notebook. "Just want to get my facts straight."

Pastor Wells tried giving Kayla the kind of look he gave me, but his powers obviously didn't work on her. She smiled and motioned for him to continue.

Which he did. " 'Because it is a theory, it continues to be tested as new evidence is discovered. Until such time as evolution is proven, it remains a theory, not a fact.' "

Kayla raised her hand. Pastor Wells ignored her. He continued to read, faster now.

" 'Intelligent design is an alternative explanation of the origin of life that differs from Darwin's view. Students are encouraged to question Darwin's unproven theory and to request and expect answers related to intelligent design.' "

Pastor Wells surveyed the class over the top of his glasses in that omnipotent way he has. He seemed pretty content with himself.

Ms. Shepherd, on the other hand, looked five steps beyond grim. "And now back to our constitutionally mandated curriculum. If you'll excuse me, I have a class to teach."

Pastor Wells stiffened and Mrs. Martinez started to object, but Ms. Shepherd pressed on. "Let me remind you," she told us, "and so you won't be confused by this gentleman, intelligent design is not science."

"As I said, it is an alternative theory—"

"Hey. Chief," she interrupted. "You had your say, now it's mine."

I'd never heard anyone talk to Pastor Wells like that. From the look on his face, he hadn't, either.

"Let's start with a definition," Ms. Shepherd said. You could see that each word hurt her, like she resented even having to open her mouth just because Pastor Wells had barged into her classroom.

"In science the word *theory* doesn't mean what it does in everyday conversation. It's not a guess or a hunch. It's a well-reasoned, PROVABLE explanation for something we see in the natural world. A theory has to stand up to testing and proof. It has to survive being challenged by other scientists over and over again. The theory of evolution has done that. It's real. It works. And let's get this straight: in science, it's not a theory's job to become a fact. Theories are there to EXPLAIN facts. To tell us why we're seeing what we see. That's the beauty of a unifying theory like evolution—it gives us a structure so we can understand our world."

She picked up more energy the longer she spoke. Like she'd been keeping it all in, ready to explode once someone jostled the plug.

"Intelligent design, on the other hand, is in no shape or form science."

Pastor Wells tried to interrupt again, but Ms. Shepherd shut him down. "I am TIRED of this particular lie. It's my duty to expose it. In this class we deal in facts.

Intelligent design is not a fact, it's a philosophy. It wants to tell us who is behind it all. That isn't science. It will never be science.

"Science is the HOW of things. It's about observation and explanations. It's not science's business to tell you whether God or Buddha or the Sky King made this earth. Science's job is to tell you what we see and let you decide anything more for yourself. Why are we here? Who dunnit? Not my business or any other scientist's to tell you. That is the beauty of this discipline. It leaves us free to decide for ourselves.

"Now perhaps we can return to SCIENCE, which is why I, personally, am here. Any questions? Yes, Ms. Connor?"

I know for a fact Kayla hadn't raised her hand. She smiled and jumped right in.

"Yes, thank you. Kayla Connor from the *New Advantage Post*. Mr. Wells—"

"*Pastor* Wells."

"*Sir*, I understand from your remarks at the school board meeting last night that you would like the subject of evolution to be banned entirely throughout the school system."

"Until it is a proven fact, yes."

"Uh-huh. So does that go for all the theories? A lot of scientists still consider gravity a theory. And what about relativity—I suppose Einstein got it wrong, too?"

Pastor Wells ignored the snickers. "I'm here to talk about Mr. Darwin," he said with easy confidence, "and his unsubstantiated claims."

"I see." Kayla squinted at him and tapped her pen

against her notebook. "Speaking of unsubstantiated, I noticed on your website you offer a book claiming dinosaurs lived at the same time as Adam and Eve—and apparently they were even on Noah's Ark. Since that defies anything found in the fossil record, I'm just curious what your proof is."

Pastor Wells wasn't nearly as cheerful this time. "As you know, young lady, I didn't write that book. But I do believe in it. I don't claim to be a scientist" (he said it like it was a bad word), "but I know there are plenty of them who support intelligent design. If not for the Darwinian agenda going on in this country right now, you'd hear a lot more about it. That's why our schools need to teach this controversy—to be fair to students and let them decide for themselves what's right."

"Well, then wouldn't it be fair to explain to students that there's no scientific basis for your claims—"

"Yes, Adam?" Pastor Wells interrupted, pointing toward the back. "You had a question?"

But of course Adam did not. This debate was already way over his head. "Uh . . . yeah. Um . . ."

Ms. Shepherd couldn't take it anymore. "That's enough," she snapped. "Last time I checked, I was the one being underpaid to do this job. Visiting hours are over. It's time to get back to work. Open your books to page ninety-five. Ms. Bailey, you will read."

For a minute there was a tense sort of standoff. Pastor Wells held his position in front of Ms. Shepherd's desk, acting as if he had no intention of ever moving. Ms.

Shepherd filled up the space right next to him, practically standing on top of his loafers.

Meanwhile, poor Hannah Bailey didn't know what to do. It's like she was waiting for Pastor Wells's permission, even though she doesn't even go to our church. He has that effect on people.

"Ms. Bailey," Ms. Shepherd repeated.

Hannah jerked into action and flipped through her book.

Suddenly Ms. Shepherd's hand shot behind Pastor Wells's back, and he must have thought she was going to goose him or something, because he jolted forward with a surprised little grunt.

With Pastor Wells off balance, Ms. Shepherd swiftly stepped into place—she might have even hip-checked him, I'm not sure, it happened so fast—and reclaimed her space at the front of the class.

"Easy there, big fella," she told the startled Pastor Wells, who was still gawking at her like she'd tried to molest him. Ms. Shepherd held up the marker she'd been reaching for behind him on the desk.

Casey and his sister exchanged a look of such glee, I thought they might actually hug.

Pastor Wells still tried to stand his ground, a micrometer away from Ms. Shepherd, like a little boy refusing to budge. Ms. Shepherd was not the least amused.

"I can't help but wonder," she said to our principal, "if the history teachers of this school are being forced to read statements from Holocaust deniers during their section on

World War II. Or whether members of the Ku Klux Klan get equal time during Civil Rights Week. Or if it's only the science department being singled out for this great honor of catering to special-interest groups."

Mrs. Martinez looked even sicker than when she came in. "We should go," she told Pastor Wells. Maybe she thought the whole thing would happen differently, although I can't see how if she knows Ms. Shepherd at all. But I suppose Pastor Wells bullied her into it. He's famous for that. All he has to do is threaten a lawsuit or a boycott, and suddenly people are falling all over themselves to do what he says.

"Ask questions," Pastor Wells boomed at us in parting. "Demand to hear both sides. God gave you brains. Don't be ashamed to use them." Then he strode toward the door like it had been his decision to leave.

Once he was gone, the whole class slumped back into their seats like the scary carnival ride was over. Kayla scribbled furiously in her notebook.

Ms. Shepherd stood silent for a moment, arms crossed over her chest, tapping her scuffed black shoe against the floor.

"Let me be clear about something, people," she began in a quiet, tense voice that intensified with every word. "I am a scientist. It is what I love. It is what I'm good at.

"Anyone who wants to ask me a question about science is welcome. I am thrilled to teach you what I know. I am thrilled to open your minds. The universe is vast and wonderful, and I want to share with you what we've learned about it. It is why I am here. I hope to fill you all with the same passion for knowledge that I have.

"But I also happen to be a lover of the Bill of Rights. I appreciate the freedoms this country stands for. So if any of you have a question about what the United States Supreme Court says I should teach you about science, you're welcome to come look at my files.

"In the meantime," she said, her lips tight and stern, "the next person who tries to mix religion with MY taxpayer-funded public school curriculum will be invited to spend the hour with their counselor looking for another class. In here we are not interested in philosophy or personal convictions. We are interested in FACTS. I am paid to teach you FACTS. Now open your books and let us go back to LEARNING."

Kayla bolted to her feet, cheering and clapping like mad. Soon Casey and Josh and the photographer and I joined in, and while Ms. Shepherd stood there practically shaking with intensity, everyone but the Back Turners clapped and hooted and yelled. It was chaos. It was beautiful. I've never seen Teresa so mad.

She just couldn't let it go. Teresa waited for the room to settle down, then stood to make her speech.

"Ms. Shepherd, on behalf of the Christian body—"

I swear, she stuck out her chest.

"—we demand you include information about intelligent design so that we can understand both sides of the controversy."

"And I demand intelligence, PERIOD," Ms. Shepherd answered. "Now for the last time, open your books, and Ms. Bailey, you will READ."

Round one to Ms. Shepherd.

But I know there's more to come.

Twenty-two

"Want to see my sister's website?"

Did I ever. We didn't have a chance to look it up at lunch, since instead of going to the library, Casey and I had accepted Kayla's invitation to brown-bag it with her and Josh outside on the bleachers and rehash everything that had just happened in Ms. Shepherd's class. Of course, I didn't bring my lunch today since I never seem to get around to eating it, so I had to bum some grapes and chips and an orange off Kayla. That girl eats enough for five.

So it wasn't until later, when I was over at Casey's house, that we finally looked at the website. We were taking a break from the project because little Orange—sorry, "Duke," since somebody bought him this morning and named him—hadn't performed so well on the airplane test. He did all right when Casey just lifted him in the air, but once he started spinning around, Duke threw up kibble all down the front of Casey's shirt.

It was colorful and elaborate—Kayla's website, not the puke—with all sorts of flashing graphics and a slide show and news clips and Kayla's daily blog (called "News-junkees' Fix").

"Wow, did Kayla do all this herself?"

"No, it's Josh. He's really great at web design. He did Ms. Shepherd's and my mom's, too."

Casey scrolled down until he got to a box marked *Joshuwear*. He clicked on it, and a selection of T-shirts came up. Under *NEW!* was a shirt saying *Proud to Have Evolved*.

"He adds new ones every week," Casey said.

"How long does it take him? To make a new one, I mean."

"Maybe an hour on the design, another hour to make a screen of it—depends on how elaborate it is. Then he churns out however many people order."

"Do people order a lot?"

"One weekend he had over two hundred. He and K were at his house inking screens all night."

"I can't believe he does all that designing and stuff himself."

"Yeah," Casey said. "There are companies out there who'll do it for you, but Josh likes to be able to turn out new shirts overnight. Plus, this way he gets to keep all the profits."

Casey scrolled through some of the designs. "He takes a lot of quotes off the news. As soon as someone says something stupid, Josh can have a shirt on the website within an hour. Like this one from Senator Bartlett last month—about how military pride doesn't equal gay pride."

If my parents ever saw me wearing a shirt with a graphic like that, with the stick figures doing—well, never mind—they'd ground me until forty years after I was dead.

Casey clicked through the archives. "He still sells a lot of his old standards. Like that one. That used to be one of K's favorites."

It sounded like Kayla: *Waiter, There Must Be Some Mistake—I Ordered a Brain to Go with My President.*

"I can't believe he does all this," I said again.

"He'll personalize it, too. Once when K was a sophomore, the school wouldn't let her print one of her articles—too scandalous. So the next day Josh and about fifty other people showed up wearing shirts that said *New Advantage Supports Freedom of the Press* on the front and *Unless You're Telling the Truth* on the back."

"Did it work?"

"No, but it did make her feel better. And Josh finally convinced her to go out with him, which I think was the real point. He'd only been trying for a year."

Casey's eyes flitted to me for just a second, then went back to the screen. He busied himself clicking through the website.

But I felt it for just that moment—like maybe Casey wasn't just talking about Josh and Kayla. Like maybe he was talking about me—and us.

But I'm sure I just imagined it. I really wish Kayla hadn't ever said anything to me about Casey maybe liking me. Now I'm all paranoid.

Not that I would mind him liking me. I think.

Twenty-three

In yoga today, Missy announced that from now on, Wednesdays will be "imaging" days. We'll only do a few warm-up postures, then spend the rest of the time lying on our backs imagining one part of our lives the way we wish it was instead of how it is. She seems to think this will help us somehow.

I have so many things to choose from, it's hard to settle on just one. Should I picture a better relationship with my parents? A world in which Denny Pierce did not set foot in my junior high, thereby ruining his life and mine? Should I imagine myself at a different high school, with completely different people, and picture how peaceful and easy that would be?

I guess those things will have to wait, because today I spent my time on something else. Someone else.

It didn't help.

Because what's the point of wishing for something— even if you wish it "vividly, tangibly, involving all your senses," the way Missy wants? Wishing does nothing. No,

I take it back—wishing makes it a hundred times worse. Because then, instead of just vaguely thinking, *Gee, wouldn't it be nice to be with this person, yeah, that might be nice*, you're thinking, *And then I gazed into his deep blue eyes, and I smelled the toothpaste on his breath, and then he leaned forward, and . . .*

I think I might have to drop yoga. Or maybe ditch on Wednesdays. This is not good for my mental health.

Twenty-four

Ms. Shepherd was sort of subdued at the start of class today, like she was just waiting for a reason to get angry. But the Back Turners simply flipped their chairs around and kept their mouths shut, there were no special guests, and Ms. Shepherd actually got to teach today.

I know Teresa and the rest are just waiting for further orders from Pastor Wells. I've seen how this goes before.

Today we covered the whole notion of sexual selection—"He who makes the most babies wins." Kind of an uncomfortable concept, but I get it. Darwin figured out that it's only the best-adapted animals—the strongest, the fastest, the best at whatever their particular thing is—who get to survive and pass on their genes.

Ms. Shepherd said, "It's like rock stars mating with actresses."

And that got us going. I'm sure Teresa or Adam or any of the Back Turners would have loved to join in, since it was such a fun debate. We started going over all the celebrity matches and mismatches we could think of, trying to figure out why nature would allow, say, an ugly old billionaire to snag a beautiful young wife. Or why a gorgeous specimen of an actor would leave one perfect leading lady for another.

Science really does apply to life.

I would never say this in class, but the whole thing reminded me of this story in the Old Testament where Jacob makes a deal with his father-in-law that as payment for Jacob tending all the sheep, he'll get to start his own flock with just the spotted and speckled ones. So Jacob, crafty guy that he is, starts steering all the speckled and spotted sheep toward the pure white ones to make sure they all mate. Then next thing you know, all the white ewes are giving birth to speckled and spotted lambs, and guess whose flock is suddenly huge?

So I'd say ancient man figured out the whole selection thing a lot sooner than Darwin did.

At lunch Casey logged on to Ms. Shepherd's website so we could see if she'd updated her blog.

There was a picture of Ms. Shepherd's white cat, Coco, crouched at the top of some stairs. Ms. Shepherd explained how she'd forgotten to clean the litter box for a few days, and Coco decided to show her displeasure by rolling her turds down the stairs.

Sure enough, if you look at the picture close enough, you can see a little something trapped between Coco's paws.

Ms. Shepherd can be so weird sometimes. Like she said, a true freak of nature.

How could you not love her for that?

Twenty-five

"I was checking out some of the creationist websites last night," Kayla told me when Casey and I were taking a break. "Get this. They say the Book of Job—"

She pronounced it "job"—as in flipping burgers. I told her it was a long *o*.

"Whatever. Anyway, there's some reference in there to beasts called 'leviathan' and 'behemoth.' The Christian militants are saying those things are really dinosaurs—trying to prove they were around with humans."

Kayla shook her head in disgust. "*Completely* disregarding everything in the fossil record that *proves* man didn't come along until millions of years after the dinosaurs were already extinct. But I guess facts don't matter if you repeat the same lie often enough."

I hated to start talking politics, because Kayla knows so much more than I do. Instead I stuck with what I know. "I always heard the leviathan was a crocodile. That's what the footnotes in my Bible say."

Kayla's left eyebrow rose. "You actually read the footnotes in your Bible?"

"Only if it's something interesting. I know that section. You think they're describing a dragon or something, but then it's just a crocodile."

Kayla squinted at me and nodded. "Interesting. You think you can get me some more stuff like that?"

"Like what?"

"You know, sort of a 'Bible Girl fact check.'" Kayla smiled. "In fact, that's it. I'm gonna add you to my website."

"Oh no, you're not."

"Make you Bible Girl. Or maybe Grrrl. Sort of a superhero for truth."

Now that part sounded appealing, but come on—me? No way was I sticking my neck out.

"I'm not an expert."

"More expert than I am," Kayla said. "All I know from the Bible is 'do unto others.' Isn't that one of the ten commandments or something?"

"Uh, no, it's something Jesus said."

"See? Bible Grrrl—you're hot. You'd be totally anonymous." Kayla clasped her hands and batted her eyelashes. "Please, baby, please, don't say no. Tell me you'll do it."

"No."

"Do what?" Casey came into Kayla's room holding a squirming Bear. He handed him over to me. "Your subjects await."

"Mena's gonna write for the site."

"No, I'm not."

"What d'ya think? 'Bible Grrrl, defender of truth in biblical citations.' It'll be a bull-free Bible zone."

135

"I don't know enough," I continued to protest.

"More than anyone else here does," Kayla said.

I was losing ground. "Can't you find someone else—"

"You should do it," Casey told me. "As long as it won't interfere with our work."

Kayla waved him off. "Of course it won't. Don't worry, you'll still get your precious A."

"A double plus," Casey corrected.

"You got it, super-geek. Mena, please. Just give me one thing—one big juicy thing that you know they're getting wrong. I know you know this stuff."

"Well . . ."

Kayla grinned. "Grrrlll . . ."

So while the three of us tried to keep Bear from tearing into Kayla's papers, I quickly laid out the whole Jacob-and-the-speckled-sheep thing—about how even back in ancient Hebrew days, they knew about sexual selection and selective breeding for certain traits. Not huge, I admit, but still, it was something Kayla hadn't heard before.

Kayla picked up her phone and dialed the intercom. "Webmaster, please report to your beloved's room." A few minutes later Josh came in carrying a printout of his latest creation: *Gravity Is Just a Theory—Why Won't They Tell Us the Truth?*

"What's up?" he asked.

Kayla pointed to me. "Bible Grrrl here needs her own section on the website."

Josh didn't ask any questions. He just sat at Kayla's computer and started coding.

Casey and I went back to the yard to work.

The puppies are getting so big. It makes me kind of sad. Mrs. Connor says the owners will all be coming for them a week from Saturday. It seems like every day another puppy gets bought and named. Now bully-girl Pink is Maggie, Blue and Red are Shadow and Pluto, and little Christmas is Elsa. I don't know why they're changing her name. She'll always be Christmas to me.

Today we were trying a few of my experiments. While Casey played with the puppies in the yard, I hid behind one of the chairs and pretended to cry. We wanted to see which of the dogs would come check if I was all right.

Bear cared—or at least he cared enough to come over and clamp his little teeth down on my wrist to make sure I was still alive. Lily cared (in a soft, licky sort of way), and so did Christmas, Shadow, and White. The rest just went on playing.

Then while I distracted the puppies, Casey went off into the corner and put on an old Halloween mask—a big rubbery thing that made him look like a hideous freak—and he rushed out growling and scooped up two of the puppies and ran off with them into the house.

Pink/Maggie went right on chewing Duke's ear, Green and Bear kept fighting over a stick, four other puppies minded their own business, but Lily and Christmas ran right to the door to see if their services were needed.

How sweet. Make that two dogs with a serious hero complex.

But Casey explained why that was bad news. "See,

in sociobiological terms, what we're really looking for is behaviors that help perpetuate the species. So if Abbey were out here and she was the one running after the stolen puppies, that would be good. It means she's trying to preserve her offspring so they can make puppies of their own someday.

"But if Lily and Christmas try to help their siblings, that's bad. Because really all they should care about is the fact that there are two fewer mouths to compete with for their mother's milk."

"So what does that mean?" I asked. "Why is that bad? They were being nice."

"Yeah, but it's not a good survival strategy. They need to be selfish."

Which was a depressing thought. I'd rather have a sweet dog like Christmas than a selfish one like Pink.

But it did make me think about the whole Denny Pierce thing. Maybe Casey's right. Maybe trying to be nice to Denny was stupid. I interfered with my whole survival.

After a while Kayla summoned us back to her room. Josh pounded out a few more keystrokes, then rolled his chair out of the way so we could see.

Oh my gosh. My very own box, down at the bottom right of Kayla's page. It was only a little smaller than the one for Joshuwear. Across the top, in yellow, it read, *Bible Grrrl Sez:* and then there was space for some text.

It was so weird. I never thought I'd have a Bible column someday—let alone on the internet, where anyone could read it. If someone had predicted this last week, I would have thought they were on drugs.

"Can you say what you told me," Kayla asked, "only make it shorter and jazzier?"

"I'm not sure. Let me think. You don't have a Bible around here, do you?"

Kayla snapped her fingers at Casey and said in a British accent, "Boy, bring us the old man's book, won't you?" Now I know where he got that accent thing.

It took a few minutes, but Casey finally returned, carrying a King James Version.

"Nice," Kayla said, taking it from Casey and examining the chewed-up black leather cover. "Tell your puppies to show some respect." She swatted Casey on the butt with the Bible.

"No!" I instinctively snatched the Bible from her hands.

Kayla gave me a funny look. "Sorry."

I was kind of embarrassed, but also kind of right— you don't treat the Bible that way. "It's just that . . . um, you really shouldn't do that. It's . . . bad."

Kayla held up her palms in surrender. "You're my Bible Girl Wonder. Whatever you say goes."

Everyone was watching as I opened it and started flipping through Genesis. "Um, this will probably take a while."

"Right," Kayla said, heading for the door. "Need anything?"

"No. Thanks."

"Okay, then, call me when you're ready." She and Josh left the room. Casey stayed behind.

"You're really going to do this?" he asked.

"Why? You think it's a bad idea?"

"No, might be fun." He settled onto his sister's bed and showed no intention of leaving. "Just be careful, you know?"

My heart beat a little faster. In part because he was talking so seriously for once, and in part because he sounded like he wanted to protect me.

"Careful of what?"

"K has a way of sucking people in. I like my sister— don't get me wrong—but just remember that this is her show, and we're all just extras."

"So you think I shouldn't do it."

"I think you should think about what's in it for you. That's all."

He got up from Kayla's bed and left me to ponder that.

What's in it for me? Why do anything that might get me in deeper with this family?

I can think of a few reasons. And one of them had just left the room.

Twenty-six

When I finished my Bible Grrrl piece, I went looking for everyone else. Mrs. Connor was out in the backyard trying to keep the puppies from devouring their mother. Abbey was doing a pretty good job of that herself, growling and nipping at them every time they went in for a nipple. Her way of saying, "Switch to solids."

I called for the others. Casey shouted, "Back here!" from the far end of the house, where he had told me his mother's office was.

I walked down the hall to the first open door and looked in. Mrs. Connor's office wasn't at all what I expected. The nice part about it is that one whole wall is just windows looking out on the garden. The sun comes right in, so you don't even need to turn on the lights. I could see Mrs. Connor sitting on the grass playing with Lily. It must be nice to be able to work at home and wear jeans and flip-flops if you want, especially if every time you take a break there are puppies around to play with.

The weird thing about her office is that for someone

who makes such beautiful furniture, she really scrimped on herself. All she has in there is a drafting table, a stool, a small computer desk, and a long conference table covered in blueprints and drawings. Other than the stool and the little swivel chair in front of her computer, there isn't anyplace to sit down. It's like she doesn't want anyone coming in and getting too comfy. And unlike the rest of the house, there are no bookcases or books or pictures or anything personal. The whole room is kind of cold, which doesn't seem like Mrs. Connor at all.

I followed Kayla's laughter to the room next door. Now *that* was an office.

All leather and wood and books and paintings and clutter and comfort and warmth. That is where I'd love to spend my entire life.

"Hey, BG," Kayla said. "Finished?"

I handed her the printout and sat next to Casey on the floor, our backs propped against the wall. Josh lay sprawled across the leather couch, his giant legs dangling over the end. Kayla had her own sprawl going across a wide leather armchair.

"Nice," Kayla said when she finished reading. "You're hired." She showed it to Josh, who barely glanced at it before going back to tossing a mini-beanbag over his head.

"We're brainstorming T-shirts," Casey told me.

"Is this your dad's office?" I whispered. Casey nodded.

I was in a snooping mood. I pushed to my feet and started looking around.

"How 'bout this," Kayla threw out. " 'If God made Darwin, how can Darwin be wrong?' "

Josh gave it an "eh."

Silence descended again. The only sound was the wooden floor aching beneath my feet as I walked along the bookcases scanning some of the titles. Soon I came to the shelves holding Mr. Connor's books.

Casey joined me and pulled out one of the paperbacks. "That's a good one."

"They're all good," Kayla said, a little defensively.

On the cover were a man and a woman dressed in flight suits, like air force pilots. In the background was the spaceship they had crash-landed. *Red Horizon*, by Jack Connor.

"Wow. That's really cool," I said. "How many did he write?"

"Thirty-nine."

"Plus all his articles." Kayla pointed to the bottom shelf, where there was a whole row of scientific journals.

"Was he . . . famous?"

"With some people," Casey said. "The SF crowd— science fiction."

"And the serious scientists," Kayla said, again a little defensively. "He had a lot of crossover."

Suddenly I understood that whole Science Brain thing Casey and his sister have going. I hope I don't have Insurance Brain. How sad would that be?

"You can read that if you want," Casey said.

"No, I . . . wouldn't want to ruin it or anything." I started to return *Red Horizon* to the shelf.

Casey stopped me. "We've got about eighty copies all over the house. Take it."

"No . . ." But I saw the look on his face. And Kayla's. It was like some sort of a test. "Okay, sure. I'd love to."

"Don't worry, no sorcerers," Casey said. "Just bloody battles and dismemberments. I assume that's okay." He gave me a little nudge with his elbow.

"Yeah, that's okay," I answered way too seriously. My heart was beating too fast. All because of that nudge.

Pathetic.

Kayla arched her back over the chair and stretched her long arms wide. "I'm burnt. I need a break."

Josh spidered his legs off the couch and the two of them headed for the kitchen.

Casey and I stayed behind.

"Sorry that took so long," I told him. "Want to go back to work?"

"In a minute." Casey plopped onto the couch and took over Josh's job of tossing the mini-beanbag above his head. I settled into the leather chair Kayla had left warm.

"So, how come you were all back here?"

"My mom lets Josh use it for his office when he's here. He's always helping my mom and K with their computer stuff, so . . ." The beanbag went astray. Casey retrieved it and went back to tossing. "Plus, my dad had this great computer and printer, so I guess my mom figures . . . I don't know. It shouldn't go to waste." Abruptly he sprang to his feet. "Ready?"

"Um, sure." I picked up *Red Horizon* and followed Casey back into the living room. "I don't have much time. Can we do something quick?"

Casey seemed glum—not something I'm used to from him. Not that I know him all that well, but usually he seems so up.

"You okay?" I asked.

"Yeah." He crinkled his brow. " 'Course." He slid open the glass door and joined his mother and the pack in the backyard.

Kayla came out of the kitchen chomping on an apple and carrying a box of crackers. Josh had a plate of spaghetti.

Kayla glanced at the clock. "Leave in about fifteen?"

"Sure." I hadn't even asked her to give me a ride. I guess now it's just assumed.

"Little C doesn't like it in there," Kayla said, jerking her chin toward the back offices. "Notice?"

"Yeah, I guess."

"I think it's hard for him to see us moving on. Like we were supposed to make a shrine out of my dad's office or something. I mean, I miss the guy, but he's not coming back." Kayla shrugged. She dug out a few crackers and alternated between those and the apple. "C's problem is he had this whole Gandalf fantasy going."

"Who's Gan—"

"Oh, that's right," Kayla said. "I heard—no *Lord of the Rings*. Crying shame, if you ask me. You really need to check out Aragorn."

"Mm," Josh growled. "Man-flesh." Then went right back to seriously stuffing his face.

Kayla patted her boyfriend's leg. "Don't worry, honey, I'd never leave you for him." She rolled her eyes at me.

"Anyway, Gandalf dies and everyone's so shocked because we all thought he was invincible, but then it turns out he is, actually, and he reappears even more powerful than before."

Kind of like Jesus, I thought but didn't say. I'd done enough Bible Grrrl work for now.

"Anyway, C would never have admitted it because he knows I would have stuffed his head down the toilet if he did, but I think a little part of him hoped for a while that one day dear old Dad would reappear, just like the White Wizard." She shoved in three crackers at a time. "Poor little guy. Sad, huh?"

"Yeah."

I didn't feel like being inside anymore. But mostly I didn't want to hear Kayla make fun of her brother for being an eleven-year-old kid who wished his dad would come back to life. I know she wasn't trying to be mean, but it made me feel extra sorry for him.

I joined Casey and Mrs. Connor and twelve sets of very sharp milk teeth out in the backyard. I sat down in the grass, and right away Christmas loped over to me and climbed onto my lap. Break my heart, why don't you? Then Bear noticed the injustice of a puppy other than him being the center of attention, so of course he had to come bite Christmas's ear. I rolled him onto his back and tickled his belly just to show him who was boss.

"Aren't we going to miss our babies?" Mrs. Connor said.

I didn't mean to, but I looked over at Casey the exact

moment he looked at me, and I got this lump in my throat like I was going to cry. I quickly looked back at the puppies.

In a little over a week, the experiment will be over. No more afternoons at the Connors'.

It's really too dismal to think about.

Twenty-seven

The picketers turned up this morning. Twenty-three of them with signs like *Let Our Children Hear the Truth* and *Only the Unintelligent Deny Intelligent Design* and *Darwin = Devil* and other snappy slogans.

There were news crews, too, which is why Teresa and Adam and the other publicity hounds were marching right along with their parents. Teresa wore a *Savior Self* T-shirt and jeans that looked like they were compressing all her organs and cute pink high-heeled sandals that were obviously not built for hours and hours of picketing. But she only had to walk a few steps anyway before a reporter singled her out—she is hard to miss—so I guess Teresa's face will be on the news tonight, just like I'm sure she hoped.

Besides the kids who were marching, I knew almost all the other picketers: six or seven moms, a few dads, the ladies from the church office, a couple of old guys who are always greeters on Sunday, and Pastor Wells's personal secretary. But Pastor Wells wasn't there himself, which surprised me. He must have had other important photo ops today.

The picketers knew me, too, of course, which didn't make it easy to walk past them, since they felt it necessary to shout, "God will judge you, Mena!" and other fun things like that.

Such a nice way to start the school day.

"Neanderthals," Kayla called them. She was leaning against a pillar near the entrance, looking like she'd barely slept a minute last night.

"I thought you didn't have class until later."

"Don't," she answered. "Paper. Out tomorrow." In her exhausted state she'd started to talk like Josh. She jerked her chin toward the crowd. "Yours?"

"Former."

"Scary." Kayla nodded toward a group of four men in sports coats being interviewed off to the side of the picketers. "Them?"

I nodded. They were from the church, too. Two of them were assistant pastors.

"Told you," she said. "Infiltrating. School board."

"They're running for the school board?"

"Election's November," Kayla said.

"But if they get elected—"

"Bye-bye, evolution."

We stood and watched the parade a little while longer. The woman holding the *Darwin = Devil* sign was really getting into it, pumping the sign up and down, shouting, "Keep Darwin away from my kids! Keep Darwin away from my kids!"

Kayla sighed and forced out some extra words. "Someone should break it to her that Darwin didn't invent

149

evolution, he just noticed it. It's like saying Newton invented gravity." Kayla shook her fist. "Down with Newton! Gravity's keeping me down!"

She cracked up at her own joke and couldn't stop laughing. "Ah, man, I'm so fried. Gettin' a little slap-happy." She pushed off from the pillar. "But miles to go before I sleep, huh? See ya, Mene. Back to the free press."

"Good luck."

Kayla waved to me over her shoulder. She shuffled off toward the newspaper office to do whatever else needed doing to get the *Post* out tomorrow. Meanwhile, I stayed put, staring at the spectacle.

And it really got me thinking.

If not for my problems with the church, would I have been out there picketing with them this morning? Wouldn't I be carrying some sign right along with Teresa and Adam, shouting, "Teach me the truth!" and "Darwin lied!" and getting all worked up over this?

Here's a scary thought: Would I hate Ms. Shepherd right now? Would I think she's evil for teaching what she's teaching? Wouldn't I have been happy to hear Teresa say, "Shepherd is going down"?

And what about Casey? There's no way I'd be friends with him. First of all, he doesn't believe what I believe, and second, I never would have gotten to know him. I'd be hanging out with my old friends, completely ignoring everyone else.

These are the kinds of thoughts that drive me crazy. Because it seems like all it takes is one blip in the road, and suddenly you're off in a completely different direction, leading this whole other life. Like a gene mutation, I guess, and now I have legs instead of fins.

What's weird is that it's only because I was kicked out of church that I've been sitting in class every day listening to what Ms. Shepherd has to say. Otherwise I would have been like Teresa and Adam and Jesse and all the rest of them, facing the back wall, passing notes during class, purposely not paying attention.

And I have to be honest: sometimes what I hear is hard to take. My brain has been brought up to believe certain things—like the fact that God created us in His own image and that we're all descended from Adam and Eve. I've never had a reason to doubt that. I've never wanted to.

But then I hear the things Ms. Shepherd has been telling us, and I read what other scientists say, and I know in my heart and in my head that evolution is real, too. I have no doubt of that. There are too many facts to prove it.

So what does that mean for Genesis? Evolution says we're all descended from a common ancestor, too, but it doesn't exactly sound like Adam and Eve. So when did they come along? Were there already apes and other creatures, and then God picked us out to make us special? Or were we always planned from the beginning, human souls waiting until the time was right to be in human bodies that walked upright and used tools and could appreciate the Garden of Eden?

Sometimes it gives me such a headache.

I believe in God—nothing will ever change that. You can hook me up to a torture machine and I'll still say I believe. I'd die if I didn't have God.

But I also believe in science. Does that make me a bad Christian? Why do I have to ignore facts just to prove my faith is strong?

Pastor Wells said it himself: God gave us brains, and we shouldn't be ashamed to use them. My brain tells me there are facts out there to prove Darwin had it right. My brain also tells me there must be a way to keep believing in the Bible while also believing in science.

Not quite as easy to fit on a sign as *Darwin = Devil*, I admit. Maybe if I had to boil it down to one easy sentence, it would be this: *I believe in evolution, and I believe in God.*

I just haven't worked out the details yet.

Twenty-eight

"Read it and gloat," Kayla told me this afternoon as she dropped the latest issue of the *New Advantage Post* onto my lap. "Advance copy. All those fans out there will have to wait until tomorrow, but you, Bible Grrrl, are now officially part of the inner circle."

She tossed another copy over to Casey, who sat in the armchair across from mine, then she docked on the couch next to Josh to wait for my reaction.

Which, I'm fairly certain, involved my skin turning the color of paste.

Because here's the headline: RELIGIOUS FANATICS TO SCIENCE: LA, LA, LA, CAN'T HEAR YOU, which isn't so bad, but it's the headline on the bottom half of the page that's the problem: RELIGIOUS FANATICS DRIVE GAY TEEN TO SUICIDE.

"They're not fanatics!"

"Says you," Kayla answered.

"And he only *attempted* suicide!"

"They drove him to it, and he would have been

successful if his parents hadn't come home in time. I stand by my headline."

I glanced over at Casey. He was totally absorbed in the paper.

"Don't look so sweaty," Kayla said. "You're still anonymous."

"Like they're not going to know it was me!"

"So what?" Kayla said. "Is any of it false?"

"No—"

"Then freedom of the press, baby. That lawsuit the Pierces brought is public information. I could have found out about it anyway. You just steered me in the right direction."

I had visions of Adam Ridgeway not only slamming me into the wall tomorrow, but then taking out his pen and jabbing me in the throat. And Teresa kicking me with her pointy shoes. And a dozen other Christians banding together and stoning me with their biology books.

Because yes, everything I told Kayla was true, but no one—I mean *no one*—wants me to advertise it. A week ago, when I was feeling all persecuted and outraged, my response would have been "too bad." But today, reading the results of all that snitching (what else can I call it?), I wanted to go back in time and beat myself about the head the very moment I decided to open my mouth.

"Besides," Kayla said, "you're not my only source."

She got up for a second to point to a line about halfway down the page.

According to Denny Pierce . . .

"Oh my gosh. You talked to him? How?"

"This thing called a phone."

"No, I mean, he actually talked to *you*? Why?"

"Why not? He's got nothing to hide. His lawsuit already says it all. 'Course, it probably didn't hurt that I told him I was a friend of yours, gave him a few facts that could only have come from you—standard Pulitzer procedure. Besides, who can resist my charms?"

Which caused Josh to pretend to choke on the cold chicken drumstick he was eating.

"Case in point," Kayla said, sweeping her arm in a grand gesture toward her boyfriend and former lab partner. "How many times did you ask me out?"

"None," he said.

"Lie. Hundreds of times."

"Twice."

"Close enough. And why was that?"

Josh cocked his head. "Your innate charm and beauty, Precious?" He said the last word in a weird, raspy voice and went back to eating.

"Exactly." Kayla kissed him on the cheek.

She was practically giddy, and Josh must have been pretty giddy himself to string together more than two words at once for a change, and I'm sure the whole thing would have seemed much more amusing to me if I weren't sitting there ready to puke my guts out. Because it's one thing to have a conversation with someone where you get to unload everything that's on your mind. That actually feels great. It's quite another to see the whole thing regurgitated in print.

"Someone's going to show this to my parents," I said. "I'm dead."

"Why?" Casey asked, finally glancing up. "Don't they know all this already?"

"You don't understand how things are right now. They'll think I'm . . . I don't know, making a joke of it or something. And believe me, it is anything but a joke around our house. All they talk about is how they're going to get sued and then they'll lose the agency—"

"Wait a minute," Casey said. "It says here Denny didn't sue you."

"He didn't." I took a deep breath so I could answer him without sounding as panicked as I was starting to feel. "Look. My parents are insurance agents, right? Most of their customers are from the church. All of the people Denny and his parents sued have insurance policies through my parents. Follow?"

I sounded like Ms. Shepherd. Except I must really have Insurance Brain, because I actually understand what this is all about.

"So Denny ends up in the hospital, almost dead, and I feel so bad about the whole thing I send him this letter telling him how sorry I am, and explaining why it all happened—Pastor Wells's crusade, Bethany's big idea about converting him—all of that. And I think if I send that letter it'll absolve me somehow and I'll be free, and then next thing I know it shows up attached to some lawsuit Denny and his parents have filed for punitive damages, citing intentional infliction of emotional distress and assault and all this other stuff."

"Denny read me the letter," Kayla interjected. "Very moving. You do good work."

"That isn't the *point*," I said, although secretly I had a brief moment of pride. "The point is, now the insurance company my parents got the policies from is saying they won't cover anyone because these were intentional acts, and so all those people are threatening to sue my parents for selling them policies that won't actually insure them. Understand?"

"Okay," Kayla said, "but—"

"So my parents are going to lose their agency, we're probably going to lose our house, they're going to get kicked out of our church, which is practically their whole *life*, all because of me."

Somehow just hearing all that stuff out loud really got to me. I've known it in my heart, but it's different once you say it.

I could feel myself ready to cry, which was the last thing I wanted to do, especially in front of Casey. I needed a break. I bolted out of the chair and escaped through the front door.

Casey has this bad habit of following me when I'm in a terrible mood. There he was again, just standing off to the side while I paced up and down his driveway.

Finally he broke the silence. "This isn't your fault."

"Of course it's my fault!"

"Why, because you wrote that letter?"

"No, because I let them torture Denny in the first place."

"I didn't realize you were the team boss," Casey said.

"I could have at least done *something*. I just went along with it—the notes, the phone calls—"

"Did you do any of that yourself?"

"No—"

"Then I don't see how it's your fault."

I stopped pacing and glared at him. "I let them do things, do you understand? Adam and Teresa and Jesse—really hateful things. And Bethany dropping to her knees in the hallway every time she saw Denny and praying to God to save his soul—how would you like that? And you know what? Some of what they did was kind of funny. I actually *laughed*. And then Denny tries to kill himself—"

"You didn't do any of it. They did."

He wasn't getting it at all. "Look, I am a pig. I am an evil human being. I could have done something and I didn't. Okay? I just let it go on."

"Okay," Casey said, his voice finally as stern as mine. "What do you want me to say? It's great that you let your friends abuse some poor gay kid into trying to kill himself? No, Mena, I don't think that's admirable. I think it's small and weak and shameful. But I think what they did is far worse than what you did, and I think sending that guy a letter telling him how sorry you were and explaining how the whole thing happened *is* admirable, and I'm willing to say so to your face. Now can we please go back inside and stop yelling since all this is futile since it's already in print and my sister is disseminating it tomorrow?"

The two of us stared at each other, both breathing a little hard.

"So you agree I'm a pig," I said.

"Yes. A huge, undignified porker. Satisfied?"

I cracked the smallest of a smile.

"Seriously, Mena, you have to have thicker skin than this if you're going to play with my sister. I told you she takes no prisoners. If you're going to sign on for this Bible Girl blog thing, you need to do it at your own risk."

"What risk?" Kayla shouted from the house. "It's gonna be great!" She was standing just inside the screen door. She had been listening the whole time.

Kayla opened the door and ushered me back inside. "Your problem is you're still thinking like Mena. Mena's nobody—no offense. That's your Bruce Wayne. You're Bible Grrrl now. She ain't afraid of nobody."

Sometimes I have no idea what these people are talking about. "Bruce what?"

Kayla handed me a semi-melted ice cream sandwich and licked the remnant off her hand. "Sorry it's a little mushy. Thought I should wait till the end of your tirade. Feel better?"

I wasn't ready to talk. I peeled off the wrapper and took a humongous bite.

"Wow, you weren't kidding—you really are a pig." Kayla draped her long monkey arm across my shoulders and led me back to the forested living room.

Josh waited until I sat down. Then he pulled out a sunflower yellow T-shirt from behind the sofa cushion and tossed it across to me.

"Your bat suit," Kayla said. "Wear it proud."

On front, in navy blue letters, Josh had put:

BIBLE GRRRL SEZ: HAVE FAITH—EVEN RELIGIOUS FANATICS CAN EVOLVE

Then in smaller print: *Join the discussion at . . .* and it listed Kayla's website.

"I can't wear this!"

"Why?" Kayla asked.

"First of all, let me remind you once again—I don't know *anything*. I am not an expert. That whole Jacob and the sheep thing is a fluke, and it's not that great to begin with."

"Says you."

"I'll probably never come up with anything else."

"I have faith," Kayla said. "Is there a second?"

"Yes. Second, if I wear this, everyone will know I'm Bible Girl." I couldn't bring myself to growl out the "Grrrl" like Kayla does.

"Not if Josh and C and I and twenty or thirty other people are wearing them."

"Twenty or thirty people? Come on!"

She counted them off. "Everyone from the *Post*, Josh's buddies, Ms. Shepherd's assorted fans—in fact, sweetie," she told Josh, "we might need a lot more. How many yellows do you have?"

"Hundred," he answered.

"Print 'em all."

"Kayla!" This was getting seriously out of hand.

But she waved off any further objections from me. "This is advertising, Bible G, plain and simple. It's how we get the word out. And I happen to think Bible Grrrl will be a draw to my website. Now wear it proud and fix your hair tomorrow, no offense."

I glared at her, to no effect. I turned to Casey, who just shrugged. He probably knows better than anyone how his sister can just wear you out.

"Fine," I said with a huge sigh. "I'll wear the stupid shirt."

"Excellent," Kayla said. "And don't you worry about hurting Josh's feelings by denigrating his product. Little brother? Size dwarf?" She tossed him his own shirt.

He held it up to his chest and said in British, "For England and St. George."

I don't know how I got mixed up with these people.

But I do know one thing: my mother had better let me call in sick tomorrow, or this is only going to get worse.

And by the way, did Casey actually say he admires me?

Twenty-nine

I have a serious problem. And it's bigger than the fact that all the people at this school who already hated me now REALLY, REALLY hate me. There's nothing I can do about that anymore. They've read the paper, they've seen my shirt, they know I'm part of some other crowd now— some movement against them and for Ms. Shepherd and for Denny Pierce and for evolution and who knows what all I haven't even decided I'm for that they're against. I guess time will tell.

The problem I'm talking about is solely within my own control to fix. So that should make it easy, right? Just decide not to think a certain way about a certain person anymore, and bingo, I'm cured.

What happened was this: he walked into biology.

No, back up.

First of all, it's lunchtime right now, and I'm hiding in the girls' bathroom because I can't face Casey at the moment, although I'll probably meet him in the library in a while just so he doesn't think I'm avoiding him or anything. I just need a break. To pull myself together.

So far, today has been just as horrendous as I knew it would be. By the time I got to school the *Post* was everywhere, in everyone's hands, and people saw my shirt and knew I had something to do with it, and just when I was wondering if Kayla had tricked me somehow and I was the only one wearing this bright yellow shirt with the big blue letters across it, I saw off in the distance, walking up from the parking lot, a group of about seven or eight people wearing the shirt, too, and I almost wanted to run to them and say, "You are my people!" but I held back, since I didn't know a single one of them.

And then I walked into English, and Bethany and Teresa sat hunched over their copy of the *Post*, and Bethany looked like she was crying, and I scurried by them to get to my seat, and next thing I knew Teresa had pitched a note onto my desk saying, *R U fricking crazy U BITCH!*

So you can guess how fun that class was.

Then I had to walk the halls with everyone gawking at me until I could escape into yoga, and that class was all right, except that I forgot my yoga clothes at home. Trust me, trying to relax while seeing in the mirror my bright yellow shirt screaming *HAVE FAITH—EVEN RELIGIOUS FANATICS CAN EVOLVE* was next to impossible, no matter how many cleansing breaths Missy had us take.

Fine. Another walk through the halls, and at least this time there were more yellow shirts everywhere. Sometime during first and second period Kayla and Josh must have finished handing out all hundred. At least I didn't feel so alone and exposed anymore.

But then I walked into biology, and Casey wasn't there yet, and for a minute I panicked, thinking maybe he wouldn't show up today for some reason. And then the door opened and in he walked, looking especially good in that yellow shirt with his dark curly hair and dark eyebrows and those eyes like dark blue lake water, and that's when it happened.

He saw me. And his eyes changed.

They went from being open and curious and ready to take it all in like they always are to suddenly looking all soft and sleepy and—I know it sounds weird but—tender. The skin at the edges of his eyes crinkled just slightly, like he was beginning to smile but didn't want to rush it. And his lips curved up just the barest amount, like the look between us was a secret we shouldn't give away. And for that one moment it was like I was the only person in the room as far as he was concerned, and he was so happy to see me, and what's more, he fully expected me to be as happy to see him, which I was. And that's how I knew.

And maybe I knew it before, like yesterday when he was sort of yelling at me but also sort of complimenting me, or maybe I knew it before then, since every time I accidentally even brush against his shirt I feel like I might accidentally pass out, but I just haven't wanted to deal with it because I CANNOT like Casey Connor. Not as a boyfriend. Why?????

1. I am not allowed to date for another year and a half. Okay, a year and five months. So having a deep crush on someone right now is a useless, potentially tortuous situation. I need to just get him out of my mind. It will only hurt to think about him.
2. I really, really like having Casey as a friend. And if I start thinking I'm in love with him, then I'll act all weird around him, and it won't be easy and fun anymore, and I'll ruin everything. I can't afford to lose the one friend I have right now.
3. It's bad enough that I've lied to my parents about who Casey is. My only salvation is that I won't have to lie anymore starting next weekend. The project will be over, I'll be back to coming straight home after school, I'll just be seeing Casey in school—the danger of exposure will be over. If I try to extend the lie by secretly spending time with Casey, knowing I LIKE him, then for sure I'll be found out one day, and then my parents will lock me up for good and never, ever trust me again.
4. I don't even know if Casey feels the same way. I think he might, but I don't know for sure. And even if he does, so what? That doesn't mean everything will work out perfectly. And even if we were totally, mutually in love, that might end someday, and then I'd have lost him forever. See number 2 above.
5. I've never had a boyfriend before. I don't even

know what to do. My parents are right: I'm not ready, and I won't be ready until I'm at least sixteen. And even then, I'll have to figure out how to deal with the whole sex thing (of which there will be none until I'm married), and maybe Casey would dump me anyway once he found out about the no-sex thing, and I'd be right back at number 2.

6. So just put it out of your mind. The whole thing is futile.

So I've decided to make myself a deal. You, self, are allowed to think about Casey—think anything you want, totally guilt-free—but only for one hour, one time a week. Specifically, during Wednesday yoga. But the rest of the time, it's business as usual, liking Casey just as a friend and forgetting you ever thought of him as anything else.

It's all I'm offering—take it or leave it.

And who knows? Maybe this way the whole thing will fade over time. If I know I can't have romantic feelings for Casey except during one class period one day a week, the problem is bound to die away. If you don't feed something, eventually it starves to death, right?

It will take discipline and vigilance, but I know I can do it. Besides, there are plenty of other things going on in my life right now to distract me. Obviously.

So no more thinking about him today. Put him out of your mind. Go hang out with him in the library and act normal. Go over to his house after school and act normal.

Go over there Saturday and act normal. Thank goodness I'm grounded on Sunday.

And then there's just Monday, Tuesday, and first period Wednesday to get through, and then it's yoga, and I can think about him all I want. And when the hour is up, I'll go back to being just his friend, and everything will be okay.

This can work. I know it.

Thirty

I am an awful person. That's just been proven once again.

I'm in world civ right now, and Bethany just came up to me before the bell, and had tears in her eyes, and asked, "Why did you tell?"

I tried to go with the lie that it had been Denny who talked, not me, but Bethany just shook her head and said, "I can't believe you told."

She sat back down and left me feeling like a you-know-what.

Because here's the thing: out of all of them, even though what Bethany did probably hurt Denny just as much as what everyone else did, the one difference, in my opinion, is that Bethany was sincere.

Bethany truly thought she could save Denny's soul.

How do I know? Because Bethany actually—it feels weird to admit this, considering how mad I've been at her—Bethany actually has a pure heart. Far purer than mine, that's for sure.

Bethany cries a lot. She cries for starving children in

Sudan. She cries for homeless people she passes on the street. She cries for kids we've gone to school with who have been beaten by their parents. She cries for people who don't know God.

And despite this, she's not a drama queen. She's not looking for reasons to break down. She'll be going along just fine, laughing and talking, and then suddenly some news of human misery crosses her path, and it just destroys her. She can't bear it. She wants everyone to be well and safe and loved.

She's about a hundred times better a person than her father.

If I were dying, I would want Bethany holding my hand. If I were giving birth to my child in a dark stairwell somewhere while bombs raged around me, I would feel safe and comforted if Bethany were there swabbing my brow. There's just something about her—no, not just something. Bethany is actually filled with the Holy Spirit. The rest of us may aspire to that, but Bethany actually has it. She's had it as long as I've ever known her.

But Bethany doesn't always know how to use her powers for good. She has a big mouth. She bumbles around and just blurts things out, like "God wouldn't like that," or "I'm sure Jesus will forgive you," or, in Denny's case, things like "A man shall not lie with a man. This is an abomination that leads to death. The sinner shall be tossed out of our midst and stoned."

Not very subtle.

To be fair, I know Bethany is in a hard position. I can't

imagine what it must be like to be Pastor Wells's daughter. Lord, thank you right now for sparing me.

I'm sure Bethany didn't have a choice when Pastor Wells came up with this campaign to root out homosexuality in our schools. He told her, "This is your mission, now go forth." Or words to that effect. So Bethany did what she was told—onward, Christian soldier.

But having a good heart, Bethany wanted to take it further. It was her idea not just to condemn Denny but to actually try to convert him. To heterosexuality, I mean. It's not like she was going to throw herself at him and try to be his girlfriend, but she truly believed that if we prayed for Denny long and hard enough, he would transform and become straight.

Maybe I believed it, too. I certainly prayed my share of prayers.

But Bethany took it all the way. Anytime she saw Denny in the hall, she'd instantly drop to her knees and start praying out loud, begging God to forgive Denny and change him.

People walking past thought it was funny, of course, which didn't help Denny blend in. And the look on his face every time Bethany did it—I think that's when it started getting to me that we were hurting Denny very, very much.

And with Bethany leading the charge, the others felt safe doing their own thing. Like the notes Teresa kept stuffing in his locker—not just Bible verses, trust me. Or the pictures Adam and Jesse liked to draw and leave for him on his chair. Or the things Lara and a bunch of the other girls said to his face, or what some of the guys did to him in the locker room.

And here's the thing: what if Denny isn't really gay? It didn't occur to me at the time, but lately it's been on my mind. I mean, just because someone looks and acts gay doesn't mean he's out there doing anything about it. It's like assuming just because a girl looks all butch she must like girls instead of guys, when really it's just that she prefers sports over makeup, and someday she's going to marry the man of her dreams and have a bunch of kids.

But then I've also been thinking, so what if Denny *had* done something about it? What if he had a boyfriend or something? I'm not really sure that's any of our business.

Because why should it matter whether someone's gay or not, as long as he's a nice person? It's like saying someone is going to hell just because he lives in some remote village in Africa and the missionaries couldn't get to him in time to tell him about Jesus. I think the only test in life should be, are you a nice person or a mean one?

And I definitely know that Denny Pierce is a nice person. And what my friends did to him really made him suffer. And that makes me feel worse than I can say, because I should have spoken up and helped him.

But the truth is, I never thought he would try to kill himself. And by the time I realized how bad things were for him, it was too late to do anything about it except say that I was sorry and explain why everything had happened.

I think maybe if Bethany had a chance and had a

different father, she might have apologized, too. Which is why seeing her all teary just now makes me feel bad for her. But not as bad as I feel for Denny. The whole thing is just a mess.

Look, I can't do anything about it anymore. My letter says what it says and I can't take it back, and now there's a lawsuit, and we all just have to deal with it. We can't change the past. We can only adapt and change to try to do better in the future. Which is exactly what Ms. Shepherd has been drilling into our heads every day, and what Josh's T-shirts say Bible Grrrl sez. Well, now I do say it: We all need to evolve.

I doubt telling that to Bethany will help.

Thirty-one

Kayla hugged me as soon as Casey and I walked into the house. "Superstar!"

I wasn't feeling anything close to as happy as she was. I shrugged her off.

"Tough day?" she asked.

"Are you kidding me?"

"Sorry, champ. We still love you."

Josh came out of the kitchen carrying a bowl of microwave popcorn and a bag of pistachios.

"Big doin's," Kayla told me. "Catch ya later." They disappeared into her bedroom.

Whatever. I couldn't shake my bad mood. Ever since that confrontation with Bethany, I'd been feeling like garbage. Even seeing Casey waiting for me after school and walking with him back to his house did nothing to improve my attitude, even though lately that's been my favorite part of the day.

At least with Kayla otherwise occupied, Casey and I could finally get some work done. We're so behind on our project, and time is definitely running out.

So I spent some time catching up making entries on our chart. Then we took the puppies outside and ran them through another stress and mental-agility test—this time an obstacle course of boxes, lawn-chair cushions, and empty flowerpots.

Despite our best efforts, the race was pretty chaotic. Unless it's mealtime, it's hard to get all of the puppies moving in the same direction at once. But Casey and I clapped and called and coaxed them along, until finally they got the idea where they were going.

Some of them just aren't into competition. I can relate. Shadow was doing fine, loping along with the others, but then he noticed this thing that kept following him— this long ropelike thing that wouldn't leave him alone— and he had to stop right where he was and chase it. Even when he managed to snap at it a few times, he still didn't get that it was his own tail. He kept on trying for it.

Right at that moment Pink figured out there was cheese waiting for her at the end, so she came barreling on through, clipping Shadow on her way.

Casey shouted, "Puppy down! Puppy down!" but Pink didn't care. She got to the finish line and snuffled out the ball of cheese we'd hidden inside a cup.

But once again my little Christmas was the compassionate one. She stopped and sat and politely waited while Shadow chased his tail, even pretending she needed to scratch so he wouldn't feel rushed. Then when Pink knocked him down, Christmas went over and gave Shadow's exposed belly a good sniff before she went back to the race. She would make an excellent companion dog.

She would make an excellent companion for me.

Why do I torture myself this way?

Casey and I ran the puppies through the course a few more times to see if they were learning (oh yes—Bear found a few shortcuts), and then gave them a break to relax and play on the grass.

Abbey couldn't resist asking to come out. But once she was there, all it took were a dozen sets of teeth snapping in the air as the puppies banded together to take her down, and suddenly Abbey was back at the door whining to go in and retreat back to Casey's room. Who can blame her? Those teeth are a menace.

"How's it coming?" Mrs. Connor asked. She joined us out on the porch with a fresh plate of nachos to replenish the one we'd already gone through.

Casey went inside to pour us both some milk. While he was gone, his mom asked, "How'd it go today at school? With the paper?"

"Awful. Everyone hates me."

"I'm sorry." She didn't try to tell me I was wrong. I kind of wish she had.

We sat there for a while not talking, just watching the puppies frolic. I could get addicted to that.

"Bad news," Mrs. Connor said when Casey returned. He handed me my glass. "We sold little White today."

White was the last one.

I could see Casey wasn't any happier about it than I was. "What's his name?"

Mrs. Connor wrinkled her nose. "Humphrey."

Casey shook his head. He took a swig that left a milk

mustache above his mouth. This strip of white right above his lips. I wanted to—

Stop. We're not thinking about that. Save it for Wednesday yoga.

"That's it, then," Casey said.

"That's it," his mother agreed. "All our babies gone." She stood up and patted me on the shoulder. "Hang in there, Mena. It'll get better." Then she left us to go back to work.

It won't get any better. How can it? The puppies are sold, the project is ending in a week, I can't fully enjoy what time I have left because I'm afraid I might be in love with someone I can't be in love with—

Oh, and there's the whole newspaper scandal and everyone hating me with extra helpings, and who knows what all might happen next week.

And then Kayla burst onto the porch, an enormous grin on her face.

"Read it and gloat, little Mena. Bible Grrrl is a star!"

Thirty-two

Kayla thrust a stack of printouts in front of my face. "Your fan mail, milady."

Okay, so I admit the e-mails—forty-nine of them in all—were pretty nice. Flattering, in a way. But that doesn't change the fact that what I came up with before was a fluke and I don't have anything else to say.

I handed her back the pages. "I'm happy for you."

"Happy for me? Happy for you! These people can't wait to hear what you have to say next. Bible Grrr—"

"Well, sorry," I interrupted before she finished her growl, "because I can't think of anything else to say. I quit."

"Quit? Are you insane? People *love* you. You can't stop now. We need more content right away. That's how you build a base."

"But there's nothing else—"

"You mean to tell me the fanatics and fundamentalists are right about everything? Evolution, abortion, civil rights, rights for women, sex ed—all of that? Come on, Mena, you're not thinking straight. Of course there's something you can work with. You just have to pull yourself out of whatever this mope is you've got going on." She looked from Casey to me. "You two kids have a fight?"

"No," we both answered instantly. What a weird question to ask.

"How about that leviathan thing?" Kayla asked. "Wanna use that?"

I sighed. "Too boring."

"*You're* too boring. Jeez! What's going on out here?"

Casey spoke up. "Mom sold the last puppy."

"So? We were never going to get to keep 'em all, little man. I love them, too, but buck up. Step back from the ledge."

Casey groaned and stood up. "Want anything else?" he asked me.

I shook my head.

"Would you tell her?" Kayla demanded.

"Tell her what?"

"To write something! Come on, C. Don't you want your little girlfriend to be a hit?"

Casey's cheeks blazed. "She's not my—"

"We're not—"

She waved us both off. "Who cares? Listen, BG, I don't mean to pressure you, but I could really use something fresh right away. Say, tomorrow?"

"Tomorrow? No way!"

"Your fans await. Don't disappoint." Kayla escaped inside before I could argue anymore.

And left Casey and me with that word—*girlfriend*—and both of our denials hanging in the air.

Casey sank back into his seat.

"She's crazy," I said.

"From birth," he agreed.

Then neither of us could think of anything else to say. We just stared at the puppies, and as relaxing as that normally is, this time it felt like any moment someone was going to sneak up behind me and push me into traffic.

Because it's bad enough to have Kayla barking at me to get her a new column, without her casually throwing out that whole girlfriend thing and then having Casey act so offended.

There's only so much abuse a girl can take in one day.

When it was finally time to go home, I'd made up my mind to be friendly to Kayla but firm. No means no.

But she's good. For every argument I made, she had three against it. And as hard as it is for me to understand, by the time we reached my house, despite all my efforts, I had actually agreed to give it one more try.

Which is why I've been sitting here for the past two hours flipping through my Bible, checking out footnotes, frantically trying to think of anything I could possibly say that would be of interest to anyone, including me.

At least when my mom came in to check on me just now before she went to bed, she saw what I was reading and seemed genuinely impressed. And surprised.

I hardly ever think fast on my feet, but this time I did. "I've been reading it a lot lately. And I was kind of hoping . . . could I maybe do this instead of watching those TV shows on Sunday mornings?"

She thought about it for a moment. But it's hard to deny a child's wish to spend more time reading the Bible.

"All right, but you still need to write us a report."

"Okay."

"With citations."

"No problem."

So now I have my own separate Bible Grrrl thing to do for my parents. What a weird and wacky world.

But if I can find something tonight and bring it to Kayla tomorrow, then maybe I can relax for a few days. Between her, my teachers, and my parents, I have enough work to last me until college.

Tomorrow I have to work in my parents' storeroom, but then they said I can go to Casey's—sorry, KC's—in the afternoon.

Which is good. I think.

I need to treasure this time. There's not much of it left.

Hold that thought until Wednesday.

Thirty-three

It's two twenty-five in the morning.

And I can't believe it.

I'm very, very tired right now, so I'm not sure I can really trust myself. But if I'm right, oh my gosh.

I can't be right. Someone else would have discovered this by now, wouldn't they? There are all those Bible scholars out there—grown men and women—and this is their *job,* and I'm just some stupid freshman reading the Bible on my own.

So I know I'm probably wrong.

But still. If what I found is true, then it may turn out to be the hugest thing I've ever thought of.

But I have to be sure. Because once I say it out loud, I don't know what's going to happen. People are going to be either incredibly angry or incredibly—well, maybe not happy, but at least very, very interested.

I need some sleep. I have to think this through, down to the last detail, before I ever present it to Kayla. Because knowing her, once it's out of my mouth, it's going to be all over the internet in a matter of minutes.

And on T-shirts and in the *Post* and who knows where else.

And if I'm wrong, then I'll look like an absolute idiot in front of Casey and everyone.

So I'm going to go to sleep now. And when I wake up, I'll read the parable once more, and then read it another fifty times if I have to.

I don't know if this is real.

I almost hope it's not.

Thirty-four

There wasn't enough mochaccino in the world to wake me up this morning, but I worked at my parents' agency nonetheless. It wasn't too bad—they're actually talking to me a little more lately. I wonder if it's because they're so impressed by my diligence over my science project. If only they knew.

As I rode the bus to Casey's, I still wasn't sure what, if anything, I was going to tell Kayla. I was still too groggy to know whether what I came up with in the wee hours of this morning makes any sense.

But luckily, Kayla and some of her friends had decided at the last minute to go to some political rally this afternoon, so it was just Casey, his mom, and me—and the dogs, of course. That was really nice.

Mrs. Connor fixed us lunch—these huge chicken salads with slices of pear fanned along the edges and blue cheese and walnuts on top—and we ate with her in the kitchen while she told us about the new wing of the art museum she's designing. Then Casey and I went to his room to spend some time graphing out the puppy results.

I was lying on his floor coloring in the bar graph when I noticed Casey kept looking over at me, then looking away. Then he'd clear his throat, go back to working on some calculations we're going to need, then a few seconds later he'd be back to looking at me.

Finally he spit it out. "Have you, um, had a chance to look at my dad's book yet?"

I felt like such a jerk. I hadn't even looked at the first page. "Oh no. I'm really sorry. I've been so busy—"

"No problem, no problem." He looked like he wished he hadn't asked me.

And maybe it's because I felt so guilty that I fell for what he did next.

I was busy coloring in the green bars for Green (now known as Smoky) when I saw Casey out of the corner of my eye fiddling around near his TV.

I let it go on for a bit longer before my antennae went up and I understood what he was doing.

"Oh no."

"Come on," he said. "Just one scene."

"No way!"

"Mena, I promise it won't corrupt you. It's this really cool scene with a horse. You'll like it." He loaded the DVD and scrolled through the menu. "It's from the second movie, but you don't need to have seen the first one to understand it. I just thought you might like it, since it's about animals."

I got up and stood near the door, ready to make my escape. But I admit I was curious.

Is not saying no to something the same as saying yes?

The scene started with some old guy with long white hair standing out in a meadow and whistling. I laughed because the whistling sounded so weird, but Casey frowned and I stopped.

And then the most beautiful thing happened. This gorgeous white horse came galloping across the field—in slow motion, so it looked especially stunning—with its long white mane and white tail flowing out behind it. And it came right to the old man (Gandalf, I now know), who said the horse was called Shadowfax, which is an odd name, but there's no denying the horse was spectacular.

Casey paused it at the end of the scene. "Want to see another one?"

I shrugged, which isn't exactly a no.

He switched to a scene where some guy with a couple days' growth of beard (Aragorn—HOT—I can see what Ms. Shepherd and Kayla are talking about) is in a stable watching some brown horse go nuts. And Aragorn steps up and talks softly to the horse in a strange language, and the horse settles down. Then this woman with long blond hair (Éowyn—I'd like to be her) tells Aragorn the horse's name is Brego, and it used to belong to her cousin, who died in battle. And Aragorn says to set Brego free, since the horse has seen enough of war.

Then Casey skipped ahead to this scene where Aragorn is passed out, floating on his back down a river, and he washes up on the bank. And some ethereal woman with pointy ears (Arwen—don't really want to be her,

185

although she is beautiful, but I still like the other woman better) kisses him (which is, I guess, one reason to be her). But it turns out it's just a dream, and her lips fade away and morph into horse's lips, and it turns out to be Brego, and he's come to save Aragorn. The horse kneels down and Aragorn grabs his mane and struggles to climb on his back, then Brego stands and carries Aragorn back to the castle and his friends.

And if you're going to watch those scenes, you might as well watch some more, and one thing led to another, and next thing I know, it's a couple of hours later and I'm sitting on the floor next to Casey, propped up against his bed, and Kayla's standing in the doorway yelling, "Mom! Casey's giving Mena drugs!"

There were two girls standing in the hallway behind Kayla, one with rust-colored hair and a ton of freckles, and a kind of stocky girl with short brown hair and glasses. They craned their necks to look into Casey's room. They seemed particularly intrigued by the hanging jackalope.

"What are you talking about?" Casey demanded. "We're not doing drugs."

"Same difference," Kayla said. "I thought Mena's not supposed to watch *Lord of the Rings*. Shape up. We need to keep Bible Grrrl pure."

"Kayla!" I looked from her to her friends. She had called me Bible Grrrl, right in front of them.

"Don't worry, they're cool. They already know."

"I thought you said I was anonymous."

"To the world," Kayla said as if it were obvious, "not to

186

the inner circle. Listen, we're having girls' night—pizza and Michael Moore with a Clive Owen chaser. Wanna join us?"

"No, thank you."

Kayla shrugged. "Fine, hang with the geek. But don't lose your innocence over this, Bible Grrrl. You need your standards."

Casey stood up and went to the door. "Thanks for stopping by." He shut it in her face. We heard laughter on the other side. "Sorry," he said to me.

But I was already on my feet. "She's right. I should go." It was like Kayla had just caught us doing something seedy. "Can you . . . do you think your mom can give me a ride home? I don't think Kayla—"

"Sure," Casey said, but then he hesitated. "You can . . . stay if you want. We can get our own pizza—"

"No. I should go. I'm still sort of on restriction." Which was kind of a lie. True, I am still grounded in some ways, but my parents are making a total exception for this project. And since it's not a school night and I told them we still have so much to do, they agreed I didn't have to be home for dinner tonight.

But I wasn't telling Casey any of that.

Because I know a sign when I see one. Kayla's reminder about my integrity was more than just a coincidence. It was a message from above telling me to stop sitting on the floor next to Casey and letting my arm brush against his and smelling how nice his hair smells and barely even paying attention to the movie most of the time—which I shouldn't even have been watching in the first place—because I was too busy holding my breath waiting for something to happen that I'm not supposed to be wishing would happen anyway.

I'd been busted.

Casey looked disappointed I was leaving, but I'd already gone much further than I should have. We had watched practically all of *The Two Towers*—which, I have to say, from the parts I paid attention to, is a really good movie that doesn't seem the least satanic. I'm sure if I stayed longer, Casey would have talked me into watching *The Fellowship of the Ring* to catch up, and then there'd be no going back—I'd have to watch *The Return of the King* someday to see how it all ends. This is how temptation traps you.

Casey and I found his mother sitting on the stool in her office, hunched over a set of plans on her drafting table. She seemed happy for the interruption and agreed to give me a ride. "You coming, honey?" she asked Casey.

"No," we both said quickly. I had already explained to Casey that my parents are strict and so I was pretending Kayla was him, just so they wouldn't get nervous. He seemed to think that was funny.

"Okay, well, I'll see you at school," I said. I felt a little relieved. I definitely need the Sabbath off from Casey. I can't keep hanging around him like this if I'm ever going to get him out of my system. Not that that will be a problem, starting next Saturday. It's just the time in between I need to worry about.

On the way home Mrs. Connor and I chatted about the dogs and confessed which ones are our favorites. I like Christmas and Bear—Christmas because she's the sweetest thing on earth, and Bear because he's just such a fun-loving brat. Mrs. Connor prefers Lily and Blue, who she can't get used to calling Shadow because Blue already seems like a good name. But we both agreed we'll miss each and every one of them every day.

As she pulled up in front of my house, Mrs. Connor said she hoped I'd enjoyed my day. "You know you're welcome anytime. My kids really like you." She elbowed me gently. "Me too."

"Thanks." It felt good to hear that, but it hurt at the same time, knowing I won't be back after next week.

Mrs. Connor glanced toward my house. "I feel like I should come in and introduce myself to your parents."

"Oh . . . um, no, that's okay. They're really shy."

The last thing I needed was Mrs. Connor telling my parents, "Oh, my son has been having such a good time with your daughter!"

Cue my parents choking to death.

I needed to change the subject. "Um, I meant to tell you, I really, really love your house."

"I do, too," she said. "There's so much of Jack in it."

I didn't know what to say to that. So I just told her good night and got out.

I have *got* to start reading *Red Horizon* tonight. I feel like I owe it to all of them.

Thirty-five

Even though I've spent enough time reading the Bible lately to write a dozen reports for my parents, I know the one I *won't* be writing for them this morning is the thing I'm writing for Kayla's website. Because my parents would not understand.

No, they'd understand. They'd just be very unhappy.

So when they left for church this morning, I quickly knocked out my report on the prodigal son for them, then went back to working on my Bible Grrrl piece so I can show it to Kayla tomorrow.

Because I'm sure now about what I read. I've thought it through and I know I'm right.

Which makes me nervous, but that's not a reason not to do it. In fact, there's an argument to be made that everything that's happened to me and the people I've met in the past few weeks—Casey and Kayla and Ms. Shepherd—have led me to exactly this moment, and that this is my destiny, if you want to call it that. I think God has called me to do this.

So I'll spend my church time this morning writing the piece as well as I can, and then I'm going to put it out of my mind. What will happen will happen.

And then I can spend the rest of the day doing homework and reading *Red Horizon*.

This might be the best Sunday I've had in weeks.

Thirty-six

Well, that didn't take long. The gossips at church work just a little slower than the internet, but they can still get the job done.

It took me only a fraction of a millisecond to know what was going to happen once I saw my mother standing in my doorway holding a copy of the *Post* that someone had given to her at church.

"THIS is that Kayla Connor girl?" she said, slapping the front page.

I'd forgotten Kayla's name was on it.

I did the best I could explaining everything—how Kayla's just a reporter, she has to write the stories assigned to her (luckily my parents didn't notice she's also editor in chief), blah, blah, blah, but it didn't do any good.

So.

1. I am hereby forbidden to have anything more to do with "that Kayla Connor girl."
2. I am hereby forbidden to do any more work with

her on my science project, even though I explained that I have to because the puppies are hers, but my parents say too bad, find another project.

3. I am from now on required to associate only with members of our church (as if) or with other people of "similar belief" to ours, and my parents will from now on be calling the parents of such potential, nonexistent friends to interview them and make sure they are the kinds of people with whom I should associate.

4. From this day forward my life will irrevocably, irretrievably, monumentally SUCK.

Thirty-seven

I didn't have the heart to tell Casey I have to abandon our project. Instead, when I ran into him in the hall outside biology this morning, I put on a fake smile and went with "Hey, your dad's book is *amazing*."

Casey smiled. He almost looked relieved. "You liked it, huh?"

"I *loved* it. I still have to finish it tonight, but that whole Catrina and Will thing with the starfire, and the battle with the Weavers—I can't believe your dad could even write all that."

My heart wasn't in it—even though it really is a good book. How can you talk about science fiction when your real world has just been hit by an asteroid? But even if I had been ready to spill my guts to Casey just then, I didn't get the chance, since once he opened the door all we could focus on was the Back Turners' new display.

There they sat, all in a pod, wearing their own matching T-shirts—neon green, fairly hideous—with their own snappy slogan: *JESUS SEZ: HAVE FAITH—EVEN SCIENTISTS CAN BELIEVE*.

What a rip-off.

Ms. Shepherd sat at her desk drinking her venti Starbucks and ignoring them while she flipped through a science journal.

But this time when the bell rang and Ms. Shepherd called out in her most bored voice ever, "Evolution," nothing happened.

The Back Turners stayed forward.

That got Ms. Shepherd's attention. "Ah, I see. An evolution in tactics. Variation and adaptation. Good. Maybe I won't have to give you all zeros today."

Teresa raised her hand.

"Yes, Ms. Roberts?" Ms. Shepherd asked nicely. "You have a question about SCIENCE?"

"Even if evolution is true, that still doesn't explain how it all started. Someone or something had to create the first . . . thingamajigger."

"Atom?" Ms. Shepherd suggested. "Proton? Organism?"

"Yeah," Teresa said, bored with the details, "whatever. That still doesn't say who created the universe in the first place."

"Excellent point," Ms. Shepherd said, which surprised Teresa. "And let us first reiterate the class policy of upholding the separation of church and state. That said, does anyone want to venture a scientific explanation for the origin of the universe?" She scanned the room.

Of course Casey's hand shot up.

"Mr. Connor. Four thousand words or less, please."

And so Casey started rattling off this long explanation

that I can't even begin to remember, but it involved atoms and subparticles and quarks and collisions and waves and whatnot. And I just sat there watching his mouth move, listening to the sounds coming out of it, growing more and more depressed because I suddenly realized with blinding clarity that there is no way on earth Casey Connor will ever consider me for a girlfriend when I am so obviously, desperately beneath him. I mean, come on! Anyone can see that. What was I thinking?

When Casey finished his recitation, Ms. Shepherd thanked him and told him he was two hundred eighty words over, but she understood it was a difficult thing to condense.

Teresa raised her hand again. "He didn't say WHO created it. That was the question."

"As you may remember me explaining once before," Ms. Shepherd said, "science is the how of things. It's the raw mechanics. The who and why of all things, we leave to other disciplines."

"But what do YOU think?" Teresa challenged, and I could see from the smug look on her face that this was the whole point of the confrontation. She must have been told by Pastor Wells to try to tie Ms. Shepherd down—force her to say she doesn't believe in God.

Ms. Shepherd is no idiot. "The taxpayers of this community do not pay me to discuss my personal views. I share personal views on my own time. In here, I teach facts. And one fact you may have noticed on the syllabus," she said to the class at large, "is that today is the last day of our unit on evolution. Put away your books, pull out paper and pencil. Time to see what you've learned."

Groans all around. I noticed Teresa wasn't happy at all. Ha. She knew she was looking at a big fat F.

I was just bending down to put my book in my backpack when Casey nudged me with his knee. I wasn't expecting him to touch me. I practically hit my head on the desk.

"What'd you think?" he whispered. "About my explanation?"

"Oh yeah—it was great," I whispered back, smiling weakly. He is so clearly out of my league.

It's hopeless.

Here I've been worrying about what I should do to back off from Casey and not get in too deep, when obviously I haven't got the slimmest chance with him anyway. He must view me as some kind of lab partner charity case. It's not like Josh getting paired with Kayla. Of course he wanted to be her boyfriend afterward—they both have freakish mega-brains.

But as painful as it is, I guess the upside of finally understanding the truth is that I don't have to torture myself anymore. I still like Casey—there's nothing I can do about that right now—but at least I don't have to worry about hurting his feelings one day when he asks me to be his girlfriend. What a joke.

I am such an idiot. But it's better to realize that now than before I do something truly ridiculous like ever letting Casey know how I feel.

We took the quiz and I think I did all right. It's weird to think that was it—all this evolution stuff has come to a close. I mean, it's still out there—those men from the church might get elected to the school board, and then who knows what might happen. I read in the *Post* that none of the other science teachers are planning to teach evolution until later in the semester. I guess maybe they're waiting to see what happens. I suppose there will be Back Turners in those classes, too, and the whole protest will continue for however long people want to keep it up. But for our class, looks like it's over.

All these endings—the puppies, evolution, Casey.

As I gathered up my stuff at the end of class, all I could think about was how I was going to have to break it to Casey at lunch that I can't help him finish our project. Either I'll get partial credit for what I've already done, or I'll have to go think up some new project that I can do without ever stepping foot in Casey's house again.

But then as if all that wasn't bad enough, I'm heading for the door when Ms. Shepherd says, "Ms. Reece, can I have a word?"

Thirty-eight

"I understand from the earful I got this morning," Ms. Shepherd said, "that I am to reassign you to a new science mentor. I didn't realize we had science mentors at New Advantage."

"I—"

"Or that Ms. Connor had volunteered. How generous—I'll have to thank her. In the meantime, my instructions are to pair you with someone—how did Mrs. Martinez put it?—mature, noncontroversial, et cetera. So, I'm open to suggestions, since you seem to know more about this mentoring program than I do."

The thing is, she didn't seem mad. She wasn't smiling, but she also wasn't glaring at me with those death-ray eyes like she'd given Pastor Wells. Not that what I'd done was even a tenth as bad as him coming in and trying to take over her class. But still, Ms. Shepherd probably had the right to be angry.

I proceeded cautiously. "Um, here's the thing. . . ." I explained that there'd been some trouble at home because of some of the people from my church. "The Back Turners—you know, the people from in here . . ."

"I read the *Post*, Ms. Reece. Consider me informed."

And then I rattled it off as fast as I could—Casey's and my project (I didn't tell her what—I wasn't going to spoil it for Casey); the fact that my parents wouldn't want me going over to a boy's house, even if it were perfectly innocent and in pursuit of science (to which Ms. Shepherd said, "Good thinking. Scientists are notorious playboys"—not sure if she was joking); Kayla coming up with the KC thing—

Ms. Shepherd held up her hand to stop me. "Let's cut to the chase." Kids from her next class were already streaming in. "One, lying is for the weak-minded. If you can't think of a truthful way to solve your problems, you're not thinking hard enough. Two, it's a good semester when I have very little interaction with the administration. In the last two weeks I've enjoyed far too much of it. Can you assure me this will be the last time Mrs. Martinez hears from your parents?"

"Oh yes." Although I really had no way of knowing if that was true.

"Do you feel you need a mentor for this class?"

"No, ma'am."

"Are you satisfied with your lab partner assignment?"

"Very," I blurted out before realizing how eager and dorky that must sound. I was secretly glad Ms. Shepherd didn't ask Casey the same question. Who knows if he'd take the opportunity to get reassigned to somebody even close to his brain capacity?

"I don't usually do this," Ms. Shepherd said, "because I prefer people to serve me of their own volition, but I am hereby sentencing you to bring me one Starbucks confection—I particularly like the pumpkin scones, but you can choose what you like—on your first day of your senior year. Fair enough?"

I couldn't tell if she was kidding or not, but I thanked her anyway and got the heck out of there.

I wonder if Josh is serving out some sentence, bringing Ms. Shepherd coffee every day. I'll have to ask Kayla.

If I ever talk to her again, that is. Right now I'd say the prospects are slim.

Casey's probably wondering where I am. This bathroom is the nicest one I've found—it only has two stalls, but there's actually a chair near the door where I can sit and write. I'll probably be spending a lot of time in here in the coming months, since once I bail out on this science project, Casey will probably be spending his lunch hours with someone else.

Someone smarter and prettier than I am, not that that will be so hard to find.

I have to go give him my Bible Grrrl thing to give to Kayla. And then I guess it's goodbye.

Thirty-nine

NEWSJUNKEE1: Hey, BG, checked out the website
yet? You're going to LOVE IT!!! You're a GENIUS,
plain and simple—love what you wrote. Hope
you don't mind—spiced it up a bit—nothing
radical, just a little extra flava. Hey, what's with
lil bro telling me you can't come play with us
anymore? Anything I can do?
MENA@REECEINSURANCE: No, thanks. Hopeless.
Long story. I'll check out the website right now.

NEWSJUNKEE NEWS FLASH!!
JESUS TAUGHT DARWINISM!
STARTLED FANATICS ADMIT THEY
WERE WRONG!

Okay, maybe that last part is wishful
thinking, but boys and girls, ladies and
gents, check out Bible Grrrl's latest! If
our own little BG doesn't set our Bible-
misquoting, antiscientific brethren into a
tizzy, don't know what will.

Is it possible that God, of all deities, actually supports evolution? Could it be (gasp!) that the finest scientific minds—minds created, some would argue, by the very God of whom we speak and who hasn't made a bad product yet, to hear it told—are actually right, and the earth didn't just spring up 10,000 years ago, complete with mankind and dinos (give me a break) living side by side in harmony until death did them part?

In other words, friends, is it possible our own Bible Grrrl has accomplished what Einstein never did, and that's create a Universal Theory—this time a Universal Theory of Religion and Science—so we can all live happily ever after together in the same public schools and worship under the same Supreme Court?

Understandable if you need to take a breath and think that over.

But don't breathe too long, because the discussion's already started!

Log on now and give us your views and don't be shy. This is the big one!

I clicked on the Bible Grrrl box. I could see right away what Kayla had changed—the title and some of the text—but at least she didn't touch the parable, which is all I really care about.

BIBLE GRRRL SEZ: SCIENCE AND RELIGION UNITE! JESUS AND DARWIN AGREE!

What do *Origin of Species* and the New Testament have in common? More than you'd ever think.

In the Gospel of Matthew, 25:14–29, Jesus told the following parable:

A man met with his servants before going away on a journey. To the first one he gave five talents (an ancient measure of money); to the second, two talents; and to the third, one talent.

When he returned, he called his servants to account. The first one said, "Master, you entrusted me with five talents. See, I have gained five more."

"Well done, my good and faithful servant! You have been faithful with a few things, I will entrust you with much more."

The second servant said, "Master, you gave me two talents. See, I have made two more."

"Well done, my good and faithful servant! You have been faithful with a few things, I will entrust you with much more."

But then it was the third servant's turn. "Master, I know you are a hard man, and I was afraid of what you might do. So I took the one talent you gave me and buried it in the ground for safekeeping. See, here I give it back."

"You wicked, lazy servant!" the master cried. "Take the talent from that servant and give it to the one who has ten talents. FOR EVERYONE WHO HAS WILL BE GIVEN MORE, AND HE WILL HAVE AN ABUNDANCE. WHOEVER DOES NOT HAVE, EVEN WHAT HE HAS WILL BE TAKEN FROM HIM."

Okay, Bible lesson's over, now let's review our science.

A fundamental of evolution is the concept of survival of the fittest. Science tells us that organisms with an advantage (WHO-EVER HAS) will prosper and reproduce (WILL BE GIVEN MORE), while organisms at a disadvantage (WHOEVER DOES NOT HAVE) will die out (EVEN WHAT HE HAS WILL BE TAKEN FROM HIM).

Take a breath. You heard right. Read it again.

JESUS AND DARWIN AGREE.

And Jesus obviously thought it was an important lesson, since he taught it to the crowds again in a different parable (Gospel of Luke, 19:12–26) and then lectured his disciples about it separately when they were alone (Matthew 13:12; Mark 4:25).

Still think God doesn't believe in evolution?

Think it over, people. Join the discussion here.

Forty

A huge smile lit up Casey's face. "You won't believe the response."

Secretly, I wanted to hear that.

Because something electric and alive came over me last night as I sat there reading what Kayla had written and what I had written and what Kayla had done with it, and I realized something:

I'm not that alone.

I may feel that way as I walk the halls of a high school where people either ignore me or scowl at me, but the truth is, this world is a lot larger than New Advantage High, and there are people out there who are willing to listen to me and talk to me, and just because I'm under what might be permanent house arrest, I can still interact and be a part of something.

It will just be electronic. But I guess that's okay.

Casey had all sorts of updates for me: number of new visitors to Kayla's website, number of other blogs linking to hers, all the e-mails and comments on the blog.

"She wants to meet us for lunch."

So Kayla, Josh, Casey, and I sat together again on the bleachers, and I bummed some dried apricots and pretzels and peanut butter crackers off Kayla (no way I'd ever ask Josh—that guy looks like he needs to eat on the hour, every hour). And Kayla filled me in on the latest stats, compiled off the library computer right before lunch.

"Staggering," Kayla pronounced it.

I tried not to act too proud.

"Josh tagged you so you'd get picked up by some Christian sites, too. Even they seem pretty impressed—except for the nut jobs who say you're going to hell."

Okay, not so proud.

"Ninety percent love you," Kayla said. Josh nudged her. "Sixty-five. Still a huge fan base. And guess what? They're screaming for a live chat. Let's set it up tonight."

But that was a step too far. Because even though I might be able to get away with a quick check of Kayla's site, there's no way I can sit down in our living room, in full view of my parents, and spend an hour or whatever in fast-paced discussion with hundreds (Kayla says thousands, but I can't believe that) of strangers, talking about something my parents would have coronaries over if they knew.

So no.

Kayla grinned mischievously. "I saved the best for last."

She pulled a folded-up sheet of paper from the side leg pocket of her cargo pants. "Don't show little brother," she said, right in front of him. "He'll die of jealousy."

I unfolded the paper.

It was a printout from Ms. Shepherd's website.

I quickly skimmed through her report on some physics research about light particles and something called "spooky action," until I got to the last paragraph.

For those of you who like your science with a dab of religion on the side, check out Bible Grrrl for the latest in biblical thought. And she gave a link to me.

"The latest in biblical thought?" I repeated. "Are you kidding me?"

Kayla beamed. "Do you understand what this means? You made it onto her website—a major achievement. Just ask little brother."

"Congratulations," Casey said. I searched his face for signs that he was upset. Either he's good at hiding it or he was genuinely happy for me.

"Not that it's like getting your freshman project listed in the gallery of geniuses," Kayla said, "but I guarantee you're the only student here Ms. Shepherd is quoting this week."

"Has she ever linked to your website before?" I asked.

"Yeah, but it's still cool every time she does."

Josh said, "Bell." It was time to go.

"I'll . . . see you," I told the three of them. I couldn't believe I wouldn't be going to their house this afternoon. I had no idea how sad that would feel.

"I don't care what we have to do," Kayla said, "but we're sneaking you over to our house for a farewell dinner on Friday. You gotta help us say goodbye to the puppies."

My heart felt like it might break. "I can't. Really. I am so on restriction."

Kayla winked. "We'll think of something. Won't we, mini-genius?"

Casey gave me a funny look, then he nodded.

Okay, so whatever that means.

Meanwhile, I'll continue serving out my sentence here at home, where there are virtually no after-school snacks, no puppies, no Casey, no friendship, nothing but me and my books.

Think I'll finish reading *Red Horizon*. At least I can hang out with Mr. Connor.

Forty-one

It's Wednesday, and you know what that means. Finally.

Can I just say that second period was the nicest hour I've spent in days? To just lie there on my back in the darkened yoga room, a gray wool blanket draped over my legs, light incense burning, Missy's mystical music playing softly in the background, and visions of Casey Connor in my head. Not Casey alone—Casey and me. What it would feel like to kiss him. Or even to hold his hand.

When the lights came up, I was so groggy I almost forgot where I was. But then I had to pull it together in time to see the real Casey and act like I hadn't just been fantasizing about him for the last hour.

I wonder if guys can sense things like that.

"I finished your dad's book," I was able to tell him, so at least we had that to talk about. His father really is one of the best writers I've ever read, and I don't even like science fiction. Or at least I didn't.

"Ready for another one?" Casey asked. "I'll bring you a few tomorrow."

"Sure." So I guess we'll at least have that connection.

I think it might be some weird kind of consolation to read all thirty-nine of Mr. Connor's novels. I'll probably skip the science articles, though. No sense trying to fake my way through those.

Biology was actually kind of boring today, compared to the past two weeks. Apparently no one feels the need to protest our new unit on classifying organisms by genus and species. It's good the Back Turners know where to draw the line.

Ms. Shepherd returned our quizzes, and I actually got an A. Casey got an A plus for adding a whole separate page of explanations Ms. Shepherd hadn't even asked for.

I'm sure the brainy science girlfriend he's going to hook up with any day now will be very proud of him.

Casey slipped me a note listing the current stats on the Bible Grrrl response. I can't quite believe it. The number of visitors to Kayla's website has gone up to 4,200 as of last night. It can't be just because of me. What I wrote isn't that great.

"Library?" Casey asked as we headed out.

"Can't," I lied. Because one hour of torturing myself with false hopes and fantasies is quite enough for one day, thank you. Besides, it's very cozy here in the second-floor west-wing girls' bathroom, and so far only one person's come in to smoke, and I can write and think in peace, and Casey can go about his business mapping out the genome or whatever he's going to tackle next for extra credit.

If only.

If only they hadn't targeted Denny. If only I had stopped them. If only I had told him in person I was sorry. If only I hadn't written that letter.

If only Ms. Shepherd had put me with a different lab partner. If only I hadn't fallen in love with the puppies. If only I hadn't fallen in love, period.

If only I were a Science Brain. If only Casey liked me. If only my parents hadn't grounded me so I can't even spend this last week at Casey's house.

If only my parents had listened to me and let me go to a different school in the first place.

It's hard to know how far to go back and what to fix on that day when someone finally gets around to perfecting the time machine.

I think I want to go back to sitting with Casey on the floor of his bedroom, watching Aragorn fight the Orcs. That might have been my last good day.

Wonder if the puppies will miss me today.

Wonder if anyone will.

Forty-two

It's Thursday, and I got this last night:

> **NEWSJUNKEE1: Operation Free Mena is in place. Is this a secure line?**
> **MENA@REECEINSURANCE: No!**
> **NEWSJUNKEE1: Meet me on the jungle gym tomorrow. Lunch.**

By which I assumed she meant the bleachers, since New Advantage doesn't have any outdoor equipment. I'm never sure when Kayla is joking.

She came alone. She kept her sunglasses on and spoke in a hushed, clipped tone. "Tomorrow. Eighteen hundred—"

"Huh?"

"Six o'clock, rookie."

"Can't. That's dinnertime."

"Affirmative. You'll be having dinner with us."

"I can't."

"Say 'I can't' once more and I'll stuff your head in a trash can. Pay attention. Your cover story: New science mentor, new project—astronomy. Venus visible only tomorrow night. Won't reappear for a thousand years. Last chance."

"Is that true?" I asked.

"Negative. Work with me here." Kayla glanced behind her to make sure no one was sneaking up. "Agent Steph will be driving a white car. Repeat: white car."

"White car," I said, working hard not to laugh.

"Affirmative. Agent Steph will enter the domicile, impress the parents, transport the target—you."

"Impress them how?"

"Agent Steph a devout Catholic, wears the cross, talks the talk. Has been fully briefed as to said parents, knows how to charm mother."

I blew out a breath. "I don't know. Maybe don't emphasize the Catholic part."

"Because?"

I hated to say it, but she had to know. So I said it really fast. "Catholics pray to saints, which is like worshipping someone other than God, which is like worshipping idols. So we don't really . . . you know."

Kayla might have rolled her eyes behind her sunglasses. "Affirmative. Lose the cross. Anything else?"

"No, but . . . do you really think this will work?"

"Affirmative. Be ready. Wear something sparkly."

And with that, my secret agent was gone.

I don't know if I should do it. If my parents find out

about this one, they'll probably throw me in a closet and nail it shut and only feed me fruit leathers under the door.

But . . .

It would be so worth it if I could just see the puppies one more time and say goodbye to them. Not to mention spend one more day at the Connors'. Not to mention spend time with a certain someone.

I don't know if this Agent Steph, whoever she is, can pull it off. I have the feeling my parents will be beyond suspicious.

Have faith. Think positive. Maybe this is meant to be.

If not, I don't even want to think about what might happen.

Forty-three

Friday. Casey must have asked me three different times this morning if I'm coming tonight. I think he's as nervous for me as I am. Who knows if Kayla's plan will really work?

It's five thirty. I'm wearing jeans, my favorite top—light blue, with a violet border along the neckline—and plain white sneakers. I can't look too dressed up or my mother will be on to me. I looked for something sparkly, but that's never really been my thing. I'll bring some glitter powder to brush on in Agent Steph's car, if I ever get that far.

I've been planning it all out—what I'll say to Casey tonight. I'm going to thank him for coming up with our project, tell him I'm sorry I couldn't see it through, but say how glad I was to be able to work with him and spend time with him and his family.

I think that will come out well. I won't sound like too much of a dork.

Of course, what I really want to say is, "Casey, I've fallen in love with you. You're funny, brilliant, kind, clever, handsome—" I'd probably add a few other things after that, if my mouth was still working. I have the feeling I'd be a quivering, stuttering mess at that point, though, so for all I know I'd only get out the "Casey" part before passing straight to a stupor.

Five forty. Is Agent Steph already on her way? What's she going to say to my parents? I haven't even told them about the whole fake astronomy project yet, which is probably stupid of me since Agent Steph will be here any minute, but what am I supposed to say? What if they won't let me go? Then what, besides the fact that my life will be ruined?

Shoot. I can't just let Agent Steph ring the doorbell and come in and kidnap me. I'd better go tell them right now.

Is it wrong to pray that a deception will go well?

I do pray it. For the greater good.

Forty-four

I want to go backward and write about what happened last, but I should start at the beginning and let it unfold properly.

Agent Steph is Kayla's friend I met the other night—the short one with the glasses, who went with Kayla to the political rally and apparently ended up spitting in some guy's hair.

Not that I'm surprised, now that I know her.

She was five minutes early, and I had just broken it to my parents thirty seconds before that I was meeting my new science mentor and we were going out to look at the stars.

"No, you're not."

"Mom, it's schoolwork."

"Mena," my father said, "you know very well from now on—"

And then the doorbell rang.

Oh my gosh. She really must be a special agent, because she's obviously got the disguise part down.

She looked nothing like she had the other night, when she was dressed in flare-leg jeans and a peasant blouse and flip-flops and had a row of pierced earrings up each ear. The only thing that was the same about her tonight was her glasses.

She was dressed like a lawyer, which is what she told me later she plans to be. Plain navy skirt, white button-down shirt, navy jacket, panty hose, high heels. One set of earrings—low-key diamond studs. She even—I'm not kidding—carried a briefcase.

Not exactly an astronomy mentor's outfit, but impressive nonetheless.

"Mr. and Mrs. Reece? Hi. I'm Stephanie Lopez." She strode forward on solid legs and shook my parents' hands. Unfortunately, they were not in the mood to be impressed.

"Ready, Mena?" Stephanie asked. "We'll need to stop by my house so I can change. I just came from volunteering at Teen Court."

Which, it turns out, was true. Stephanie had been defending some kid for spraying graffiti. The teen jury sentenced him to forty hours of community service, painting over other people's spray jobs. Justice.

"Mena isn't going anywhere," my mother told her. "We only just found out about this."

Stephanie rounded on me, looking seriously outraged. "Mena! You didn't tell them ahead of time? What did we talk about? One, preparation. Two, responsibility. Three, respect." Stephanie turned back to my parents. "I am so sorry, Mr. and Mrs. Reece. This really was Mena's responsibility. I understand your disappointment in her."

I stared at her in dismay. This was going all wrong.

"Want to try again?" Stephanie asked me. "I believe an apology is in order."

"Um . . . I'm really sorry—"

"Not to me," Stephanie said. "To them."

"Oh. I'm really sorry," I told my parents. "I should have told you earlier."

"You mean *asked*," Stephanie corrected me.

I quickly agreed. Stephanie was seriously scaring me.

My mother wasn't buying it. "We've already told Mena no more extracurricular activities."

Stephanie nodded. "I understand. This is a hard stage in a teenager's life—for both the parents and the student. It's why one of our goals in the mentoring program is not just to bolster our freshmen's academics, but also to instill responsibility in them. As you can see, we have a lot of work to do with Mena."

I couldn't believe it. Whose side was she on?

And yet I could believe it. In fact, the more Stephanie talked, the more I became convinced there really was a mentoring program, and I was one of their more challenging cases.

My parents were starting to believe it, too. Stephanie was telling them just what they wanted to hear.

"Now," Stephanie said crisply, opening her briefcase. "I just have a few forms for you to sign."

"Forms?" my mother asked.

"I'm sorry Kayla Connor didn't do this before. She's notorious for flouting the rules. This will only take a few minutes."

Stephanie pulled out a manila file with my name on the tab. Inside were about twenty papers, clipped together.

"The school wants me to have these signed before I take her anywhere," Stephanie explained. "You understand— liability."

The papers all bore the New Advantage High School emblem, just as real as if someone had stolen the principal's stationery. I could only guess Josh had done some magic, downloading and replicating the design.

But the forms, I found out later, were all Stephanie. Her parents are both lawyers, and apparently Stephanie inherited Law Brain, because those forms looked as official and complicated as anything I've ever seen at the insurance agency.

"If you'll just sign all these . . ." Stephanie went through them one by one, explaining the purpose of each: emergency contact form, permission form, health information, agreement that their child could participate in the mentoring program.

The whole process took about ten minutes. Stephanie gathered the forms, promised to mail them copies, then said, "Ready, Mena? We need to be in position before it's dark."

"Where are you going?" my mother asked.

It had worked!

"There's a spot up on Prospector where a lot of us like

to set up our scopes. It's high enough that we can avoid glare from the city lights. Venus should be stunning tonight—a real treat for us amateur astronomers. Right, Mena?"

I nodded, practically hypnotized by this tale she was spinning.

"When will you be back?" my mother asked.

"No later than ten," Stephanie promised. "I'm an early bird—up at five—so I can't last much past ten anyway."

Even though the signs were there, I still wasn't completely sure I was free. But then Stephanie pulled out her final play. She handed them a business card and said, "Here's my cell phone number and e-mail. Feel free to contact me anytime this semester if you have comments or concerns about Mena's progress. That's what we're here for."

"All right," my mother said. "Thank you."

It was like Moses finally convincing Pharaoh to let his people go. Without all the plagues or bloodshed.

"Bye," I told my parents as I followed Stephanie to the door. I made my escape before they could change their minds. As Stephanie and I walked away from the house, she mumbled out of the side of her mouth, "Keep it up. We don't relax until we're out of sight."

She was on my side after all. I sort of wondered back there.

Stephanie waited until she'd driven to the end of our block before she gave up the act. Then she slumped back in her seat and smiled. "Well, that was fun, wasn't it?"

And that's when it hit me.

I had just done a terrible, terrible thing. I'd been so caught up in the drama, I hadn't thought about what we were doing.

Granted, it's wrong of my parents to keep me hostage in the house, to keep me from making any friends at all just because they're not my church friends anymore. But I couldn't help remembering what Ms. Shepherd had said. *Lying is for the weak-minded. If you can't think of a truthful way to solve your problems, you're not thinking hard enough.*

But how was I ever going to get to spend the evening with the Connors if I told my parents the truth? And it was just this one night—our last night together—and I figured I could make it up to my parents by not lying ever again. It was just this one time. Can't God forgive me for one time?

As we drove to the Connors', I put it out of my mind. I needed tonight to be perfect.

Forty-five

As soon as we got to the Connors', Stephanie changed into sweatpants, flip-flops, and a T-shirt she had stowed in the back of her car. Special agents come prepared.

It was a small party—just the Connors, Josh, me, Stephanie, and Kayla's red-haired friend, whose name is Jodi.

We ate out on the back patio and let the puppies run free. Mrs. Connor had baked up some homemade dog biscuits and gave each of them one to gnaw on. Bear finished his and stole Lily's, big surprise, and then Pink came and wrestled him for it, and it was business as usual in Puppyland.

Mrs. Connor showed us the twelve baskets she'd prepared for the new owners, complete with shot records, registration papers, a few pigs' ears, and a stuffed squeaky toy for each of them. It almost made me cry. I wished I were one of her puppies.

Abbey roamed among the litter, surveying the troops, snapping back when their little teeth snapped at her. I wonder if she realizes they'll all be leaving tomorrow. How awful will that feel?

We all ate our share of pizza—Hawaiian for Kayla, pepperoni for Josh and Casey, anchovy and bacon for Stephanie (yuck), and plain cheese for Jodi and me. Mrs. Connor sampled some of each. Don't know where she puts it, since she's about as skinny as Kayla.

And then the party sort of broke up. Kayla and her friends all went to the living room to watch some documentary on the large-screen TV.

"You . . . want to go to my room?" Casey asked me.

My heart did a little jig. "Um . . . sure."

"*Fellowship*? Or *Return of the King*?"

It was my last night. I had lied to get there. All my parents had to do was check with the school next week and they'd know Stephanie was a fake. Ms. Shepherd might get another call, she'd be mad at me, I'd be in even huger trouble at home, which is hard to imagine—really, nothing good could come of this night.

Since I was already condemned, I might as well go out in style. "*King*. I'd rather know the end than the beginning."

It was almost seven thirty. I had to be home by ten. Casey broke it to me that we wouldn't be able to watch the whole thing.

"Pick out your favorite scenes," I told him. "You can tell me the rest later."

We settled onto his floor, leaning against the bed, lights out to heighten the movie effect.

And I can't tell you one thing I saw on the screen, because the whole time my head was buzzing, my heart was racing. I kept realizing I was holding my breath.

Okay, that's a lie—I do remember a few scenes. Like the elephants attacking, and Éowyn's great line when she stabs the Witch King in the face ("I AM NO MAN!"). And this really uncomfortable part at the end, where Aragorn kisses Arwen and fully uses his tongue.

We still had half an hour left. "Want to go play with the puppies?"

I nodded. My heart hurt.

We went out in the garage and flicked on the light. The clump of puppies stirred, but only a few of them actually woke up.

"Want to hold one?" Casey asked.

I nodded. I was too choked up to speak.

We gently lifted Lily and Christmas from the pen. Christmas was so much bigger than the first time I held her. But she still folded into my chest perfectly, and breathed her soft puppy breath, and now there was nothing I could do about it—a tear rolled down my cheek.

"I'm going to miss you, girl," Casey told Lily, and he kissed the top of her soft black head.

And that's what did it.

I stared at him in utter wonder at how tender that kiss had been. Casey's eyes met mine. We both stood there, just staring at each other.

And then I don't know who moved first, but somehow

we came together, puppies cradled between us, and Casey Connor kissed me and I kissed him back.

Lily licked my chin. Casey kissed me again.

We put the puppies back to bed.

And turned out the lights and sat on the step and kissed until ten o'clock.

Forty-six

So this is how it feels.

I think I finally understand how drug addicts must feel.

I never understood how you couldn't give something up if you really tried. But if someone told me now I could never kiss Casey Connor again or else I'd end up on the streets pushing a grocery cart filled with all my belongings, I wouldn't care. Just give me one kiss per hour—okay, per minute—and I'll put up with anything.

When we finally stopped kissing, my heart was speeding like a cheetah. I started to shake.

"You okay?" Casey stroked my arm, like maybe I was cold.

I nodded. Closed my eyes. Rested my head against his shoulder.

Then he opened the door to the garage and we had to pretend that nothing had happened.

I went to find Stephanie, since I was already going to be late.

"Did you kiss the puppies goodbye?" Kayla asked me.

"Uh-huh." I purposely didn't look at Casey.

*　*　*

Stephanie brought me home, just fifteen minutes late, and I smiled at my parents and told them Venus was beautiful and I was tired and would see them in the morning.

They said they want to have a talk with me tomorrow. That's never good, but unless they somehow found out about Agent Steph already—which I doubt, or they would have said something—I don't see what new thing they have to punish me for. Think positive—maybe they just want to talk about me doing more work for them at the agency.

For right now, all I want to do is sit on the floor, my back against my bed, reliving what it was like to sit this way next to Casey tonight. And I know this is embarrassing to admit—I should probably rip out this page and burn it—but I've actually been holding my pillow against my mouth, pretending we're still kissing. Casey's lips were just that soft.

I don't want to sleep. I want to stay awake until it's morning and replay tonight over and over and over.

So this is what it feels like.

I had no idea.

Forty-seven

I don't think girls are supposed to call boys. I know we live in modern times and all, but it just seems weird to call a boy the next day after you've kissed. What are you supposed to say? "Hi, I really liked that, when can we do it again?" Or are you supposed to act all cool like nothing happened and wait for it to just come up in conversation? "Hey, I heard there was an earthquake in Turkey. What? That kiss? Oh yeah . . ."

I know for sure Casey won't be calling here. He understands my parents wouldn't like that. So does that mean I have to wait until Monday to see what's going to happen? To see if he actually likes me, or if that was just some fluke brought on by our sorrow over the puppies leaving?

I wonder which one of them will be the first to go. I wish so much I could be there today. But that would probably be torture, watching each of our babies being driven off in the hands of strangers.

Of course, I could console myself by sneaking into some dark corner with Casey and wrapping my arms around his neck and kissing him until I forgot my own name.

I couldn't sleep at all last night, no surprise. I finally got up while it was still dark outside, went downstairs, and made myself some hot chocolate because I feel like pampering myself today. I am now officially a Girl Who Has Been Kissed, and kissed well, and I figure I deserve a little chocolate for breakfast. I might declare this an annual holiday.

This is going to sound crazy, but I almost wish Teresa were still my friend so I could call her this morning and tell her everything.

Maybe I'm just being extra mushy right now, but I have to admit that sometimes I feel guilty about how it all ended with her. After the way she's been treating me, you'd think I would feel nothing but joy to be rid of her.

But if I had to be totally honest, I think I'd have to admit that I understand why she hates me. I mean, if she had sent some letter to someone apologizing for what I had done—without telling me—and then as a result my parents got sued for everything they own, I think I'd be pretty hateful myself.

BUT I can't see me ever slamming Teresa into her desk or calling her a *b-i-t-c-h* or any of that.

Which, if I'm *really* going to be honest, I also have to admit was part of the reason I liked hanging out with Teresa in the first place. It's exciting to have a friend like her who says what you'd never say and does things you never thought you'd get away with.

232

The truth is, Teresa is the same person today as the one I've liked for years. *I'm* the one who's changed. And my problem is, instead of telling her to her face I didn't like what she was doing and didn't want to be friends with her anymore, I just sent that letter to Denny and let things happen as they would. I should have been brave and up front. But instead I was a coward, and now it's caught up with me and I have to pay the price.

But I still don't have to like it.

Anyway, my point about this morning is I wish I had someone—anyone—to share it with. But what do you do when the only friend you have right now is the very one you need to talk about behind his back?

Oh my gosh. I just checked my e-mail, and there's actually something from Casey. It's times like these I wish my parents would let me get instant messaging. Our e-mail is so slow.

NUMENOR: K gave me your e-mail address. I hope this is okay.

MENA@REECEINSURANCE: Sure it's okay. What are you doing up so early?

NUMENOR: Homework. You know how it is. ;) How are you?

MENA@REECEINSURANCE: Tired. You?

NUMENOR: Ditto. Want puppy updates on the hour?

MENA@REECEINSURANCE: Yes, please.

NUMENOR: What are you doing today?

MENA@REECEINSURANCE: Working in my parents'
    storeroom. Again.
NUMENOR: Will I see you this weekend?
MENA@REECEINSURANCE: Don't see how.
NUMENOR: Too bad. Everything okay?
MENA@REECEINSURANCE: Yes.
NUMENOR: I mean, EVERYTHING OKAY???
MENA@REECEINSURANCE: YES!!!
NUMENOR: Just checking.
MENA@REECEINSURANCE: Good luck with the
    puppies. Give them all big kisses from me.
    I mean it.
NUMENOR: I'd rather kiss someone else.
MENA@REECEINSURANCE: I hear my parents
    getting up. I have to go.
NUMENOR: I'll send updates.
MENA@REECEINSURANCE: You'd better!!

Forty-eight

Please tell me I'm dreaming.

That talk my parents wanted to have with me? I wish it were about last night. I wish it were about anything but what it was.

They actually want to make some sort of Stand tomorrow at church. They told me they talked to their lawyer yesterday, and she said it looks bad for them to be slinking around, acting like they've done something wrong. She said it's industry standard to sell the kind of home owners policies my parents sold the people from church, and the chances of someone recovering against my parents if and when they do sue are pretty slim. Still, the lawyer thinks it would be a better strategy for my parents to go to church with their heads held high, daughter in tow, rather than keep acting like there's a reason to hide.

Plus, the lawyer said I have this kind of "force field" around me now, since I'm the one who busted everyone for harassing Denny nearly to death. She thinks that showing up with me every week will remind people not to push my parents too hard.

Force field? Give me a break! Is she on drugs? If anyone is going to get reamed tomorrow, it's me. I can't even imagine showing up and having to face Teresa and Adam and the holy host of youth group bullies I'm already having to suffer through seeing five days a week.

I tried to explain to my parents that everybody hates me, no one wants to see me, going with them to church will only make things worse, blah, blah, blah, but they wouldn't listen. They said I'm going.

> **NUMENOR:** Just lost Blue. My mom had a really hard time handing him over. I thought the poor couple was going to have to pry him out of her hands. They had a little boy with them, and he nearly wet his pants, he was so excited. How's it going with you?
>
> **MENA@REECEINSURANCE:** Awful! Miserable!! OMG you wouldn't believe what just happened. My parents are making me go to church with them tomorrow. They might as well prop me up in front of the firing squad. Remember how Stephanie spit in that guy's hair at the rally? Take that, multiply it by twenty—that's how people are going to treat me. And I'll have to face Pastor Wells again, too, and I'd rather lick pigeons. Tomorrow should be tons of fun. I think I'm going to stick my head in the oven now.
>
> **NUMENOR:** Ouch.

MENA@REECEINSURANCE: To say the least.

NUMENOR: Will it make you feel any better to know that when Lily's parents just picked her up, she actually leaped into their arms, she was so excited?

MENA@REECEINSURANCE: No. I hate those people. We deserve Lily.

NUMENOR: I'm really sorry you have to go there tomorrow.

MENA@REECEINSURANCE: It's part of my continual punishment.

NUMENOR: Anything I can do?

MENA@REECEINSURANCE: Don't give away little Christmas. Save her for me and put her under my tree in a few months.

NUMENOR: I wish I were with you right now.

MENA@REECEINSURANCE: I'm no fun to be with. I miss you. Talk to you later.

I deleted it all. Even though I doubt my parents would check my e-mail—they already feel pretty secure, having installed every filter recommended by the Christian sites, plus a few more they found on their own, so that I won't accidentally run off with some guy who's been writing to me from prison—still, there's no sense in giving my parents yet another reason to be mad.

Not that they should ever be mad about Casey. He's the nicest guy I've ever met. I'm sure if they were even halfway normal like Mrs. Connor, they'd be thrilled to see their daughter hanging out with someone as smart and kind as him.

But until they undergo a personality transplant, I guess I'll have to keep Casey to myself.

Which is better than nothing, trust me. It's just that I wonder sometimes if I'll ever get to live a normal life.

And if I'm going to have to keep lying like this from now on.

Forty-nine

I wish someone had been filming my life today, because I almost don't believe it myself.

All I could think about as I got dressed for church was Kayla saying, "Wear something sparkly." I read somewhere that ancient warriors used to paint their chests black before putting on their clothes and armor, because that way in battle they'd remember their black hearts and show no mercy.

This was not an occasion for glitter powder, but I thought a black bra and underwear were entirely appropriate. Because if my parents actually wanted me to sit there for an hour of church and listen to Pastor Wells talk about sinners and evildoers while glaring at me the whole time, then spend an hour in Sunday school with that den of vipers known as the youth group, and then spend another hour hanging out in the food court or the sanctuary patio while my parents attended yet another worship service—well, I needed a little armor.

I completed my outfit with black slacks, black calf-high boots, and a dark red (puce!) blouse that made it look like I wasn't afraid to wear bold colors because I certainly wasn't trying to hide.

Right.

I kept thinking as we walked up the sidewalk to the church, "I'm here to worship. I'm here to worship. I'm here for God. . . ." We entered the double doors into the lobby and immediately faced the gauntlet of handshakes from this morning's welcome team.

They were as shocked to see me as if I'd shown up eight months pregnant.

We entered the sanctuary. I tried to take a seat in the very back, but my parents were firm: we were to sit up front, our heads held high.

So we took the long, hard march up the aisle, past every ugly face glowering at me for getting their almighty pastor and church sued by some pansy gay kid sinner and his equally hell-destined parents (I know how these people think), and finally after an eternity we got to take our seats, smack in the very first row.

I've heard that at funerals, sometimes they drug the grieving widow or widower to help them get through the service. Normally I wouldn't say this, but today I wouldn't have minded some of that myself.

Pastor Wells sat off in his corral to the side of the stage, watching every step of our procession, and he looked . . . happy.

Which was not a good sign, to say the least. Nor was the fact that he started hurriedly flipping through his Bible, although I didn't understand what that meant until later.

There's a lot of rigmarole to get through in church before you actually get to the meat of the sermon. There's the part at the beginning where we stand and greet the people around us (only one person shook my hand—some old woman who probably couldn't see it was me). Then we recite some verses together, sing a hymn, pass the collection plates, sing some more, listen to the choir sing—all those things I used to enjoy. I actually happen to love church, normally.

But not today. Not anymore. I don't know if I can ever set foot in a church again.

Because while we were praying and singing and preparing our hearts for an uplifting sermon, Pastor Wells sat there so smugly and waited for his moment of glory.

And revenge.

"Beloveds," he finally began, "welcome, and praise God for this glorious day."

So far, so good. But then he looked at me and smiled. "And for the return of lost lambs to the fold."

It was the same kind of smile the hungry Orc had in *The Two Towers* when he looked at Merry and Pippin. *"What about them? They're fresh."*

"I was going to speak today on the second of the beatitudes—blessed are those who mourn—but I believe we will save that for next week, because there is something more particular I wish to speak to you about today."

I don't think my parents had caught on yet. Unlike me, they were still sitting up straight, innocently ready to listen.

Pastor Wells smiled again. That smile was broadcast onto the three huge video screens above his head so all the people in the ultra-back could see and appreciate how commanding and gifted he is.

"Please open your Bibles to the Gospel of Matthew, chapter 27, verse 3." Pastor Wells waited for people to find it, then he read aloud.

" 'When Judas, who had BETRAYED him, saw that Jesus was condemned, he was seized with remorse—' "

Pastor Wells paused and gazed lovingly at my family. I wanted to scream.

" '—and Judas returned the thirty silver coins to the chief priests and the elders. "I have sinned," he said, "for I have betrayed INNOCENT BLOOD." ' "

Pastor Wells paused to let the full gravity of that weigh on us. Then he bowed his head toward his Bible once more and read the last few lines.

" ' "What is that to us?" they replied. "That is your responsibility." So Judas threw the money into the temple and left. Then he went away and HANGED HIMSELF.' "

Pastor Wells softly closed his Bible. It was the shortest sermon I'd ever heard him give, but then again, he'd had to think it up on the fly. Besides, everyone knew what—whom—he was talking about, so why add another word? Pastor Wells's eyes shone as he gazed out on his congregation, love and acceptance on his face. At least that's how it looked on the monitors.

"Let us pray. Precious Lord, you gave of your life for us. You knelt in the Garden of Gethsemane, praying that this cup might be taken from you. 'Yet not as I will,' you said, 'but as Thou will.' "

Pastor Wells's voice rose and boomed over his lapel microphone. "Father, we come to you today with the same prayer in our hearts: not as we will, but as Thou will. We will take this cup, handed to us by the Betrayer, and we will lift it up, knowing that God in all his mercy, and the Son and the Holy Ghost, are with us now and forever, and will protect us from every harm and send us mercifully on our way. And the Betrayer will be punished. In Christ's name, amen."

"Amen," the congregation murmured in response, just like they always do. But then somewhere in the middle of the room, applause broke out—*applause*. And pretty soon the whole church joined in.

I glanced to my right and saw the look of horror on my parents' faces. "Let's go," my mother said.

"No!" I said. "Everyone's looking!"

"Mena, we're *leaving*."

It was the worst thing she could have done, but she did it anyway. The applause continued as we rose and slunk down the aisle. We were only halfway when the organist launched into her intro, and the choir stood, and the congregation joined in singing "How Great Thou Art," some of them with their eyes closed (although most people preferred to watch us) and their arms raised high, swaying in time with the music, calling down Jesus to be with them. And Pastor Wells peered at us from the pulpit and the three megascreens above him, smiling triumphantly because he knew Judas was no longer in the house and would probably never return.

My mother was crying by the time we reached the doors. I thought I might do the same, I was so angry and embarrassed. But mostly angry.

And then off to my right, in the last row, out of the corner of my eye I saw an apparition—it had to be that. I turned my head fully toward him and saw that he was flesh and blood.

I shook my head slightly and walked on as if I didn't know him.

My parents and I hurried through the lobby, then burst through the double doors, out toward the parking lot. My mother was an absolute wreck.

I knew the last thing I should do was open my mouth and say a word, but something came over me and I couldn't stop myself. "Can you BELIEVE that? Can you believe what he said? Oh my gosh, I can't believe he just did that!"

And then I started crying, too. I knew my parents were never going to forgive me after what they'd just been through. This was really the end.

My mother snapped, "Get in the car."

I got in with the two of them and sat there knowing the next words out of my mother's mouth were going to be about how I had brought this on all of us, I should never have defied the church, I had disgraced my parents, etc.

But instead my mother said, "Son of a *bitch*!"

Now, let me be clear—my mother NEVER cusses. Not even when it's justified, like when she drops something on her foot. Our household is strictly a "darn it" and "gosh" sort of place.

So hearing my mother use the SOB word was about as close to mutiny as I've ever known.

My father didn't even object. He looked as angry as I felt. But I was still sure they'd be taking it all out on me.

We drove in silence all the way home. My father pulled into the garage and shut off the ignition.

My mother turned around in her seat and fixed me with the most murderous glare.

"That was unforgivable," she began, and I was just about to lay out some defense when she continued. "That man is a disgrace to the ministry and I hope he gets fired. I'm writing a letter to the board. They won't listen to me, but I'll keep writing. I'll do whatever it takes to have him removed."

"Mom—"

"What you did," she told me, "was wrong. You should never have sent a letter to that boy—it was stupid."

"But I only wanted to—"

"You should have told us what you were doing. You should have asked us first. Do you understand, Mena? You don't write a letter like that. You don't send it to that boy. You don't put things like that in writing. They *always* come back to hurt you. It was a stupid thing to do."

I felt a little light-headed. Was that what this was all about? Not that I'd turned against the church or taken

Denny's side—was the whole war really just about me putting my feelings in writing?

But no, that was only the first part of my sin.

"And after all that, you go shoot off your mouth to that KC girl so she can put it in the paper? Do you understand what it was like to hear about that at church? We've been trying to maintain at least some *semblance* of civility there—"

"Mom—"

"I'm not finished."

All this time my father just sat there, looking straight ahead at his tool bench in the garage. He always lets my mother do the dirty work. I think it's one of the foundations of their marriage.

"You seem to think you can do whatever you want, whenever you feel like it," my mother continued. "You think all that matters is what you feel like doing, moment to moment. Queen Mena—is that it?"

"No! Mom—"

"We are a family of three, Mena. Not one, not two—three. Your father and I do not make decisions about our family without considering how they might affect you. But it seems you feel no need to return the favor."

Which isn't exactly true—my parents have made lots of decisions about my life without ever consulting me, but I wasn't going to argue the point.

"But Mom—"

"What, Mena? What? Speak. What do you have to say for yourself?"

After all those times trying to butt in, now I was speechless. But I had to come up with something. This might be my last best chance to improve the situation.

I prayed for help. And for once in my life, the answer came right away. Maybe I already knew what I had to do—I mean, obviously I knew. But knowing isn't the same as accepting it. Until that exact second, I wasn't ready to do what I knew had to be done. It was just too ugly to consider.

But then I heard my answer, echoing in my brain in Ms. Shepherd's own voice: *Lying is for the weak-minded. If you can't think of a truthful way to solve your problems, you're not thinking hard enough.*

I slumped back against my seat. I really had no choice. I either had to go on lying, or stop it right then and deal with whatever the consequences might be. I'm not good at lying. It takes too much out of me. And the bottom line is, that isn't who I want to be. I'd rather know I have some integrity, even if it means never being allowed out of the house again.

I took what felt like might be my last breath on earth. And then I began. "I need to tell you some things."

I started off slowly, trying to build a good case for myself. I told them how awful school has been. How vindictive Teresa and the rest of them are. How being friends with Casey and Kayla is the only decent thing that's happened to me in months.

"You brought that on yourself," my mother said. "You're the one who wrote that letter."

"Yeah, but I *had* to! Denny almost died. What was I supposed to do?"

"Pray," my mother said. "Ask for forgiveness."

"I did ask for forgiveness," I said. "From Denny."

"And look where it's got us," my mother said.

I bit my tongue. I could have said that God wants us to reconcile with the people we've hurt. I could have said that I wasn't the one who tortured Denny. I could have said that I thought my parents—not to mention God—wanted me to be kind to people. I could have said a lot of things, but it was obvious that arguing with her about Denny was not going to help me. Especially since I still had to tell them the rest of it.

All my lies. From that first phone call, when I didn't tell my mother that Casey was a boy, to asking Kayla to pretend she was Casey, to going over to the Connors' house every day, knowing my parents wouldn't have allowed it if they'd known.

"What were you thinking?" my mother demanded.

That I wanted to be happy, I thought, but I didn't say it. *That I wanted to be liked again. That the silent treatment at home and the meanness at school were killing me. That I was beginning to understand how Denny felt, having to face those kids every day. That until Casey invited me to his house, I thought my life might never be happy again.*

"How could you look us in the eye, day after day," my mother asked, "knowing you were lying to us?"

I just shook my head. The lump in my throat was the size of the moon. I knew I still had to tell them more.

"Um . . . Stephanie? She isn't really my mentor. That was just so I could go over to Casey's house—so I could say goodbye to the puppies."

The look on my mother's face was something I never care to see again. It was a mixture of rage and sadness and confusion. Her lips got small. Her eyes watered. I didn't want to keep talking, but I had to confess it all.

People say it feels good to tell the truth, to unburden yourself. It doesn't. It felt like I was boiling myself alive. Because with each word out of my mouth, I knew I was pushing myself further and further away from that day when I would ever regain my parents' trust. Which meant I was that much further from ever having a normal life again.

My mother was absolutely speechless. She stared at me while my father stared at his tool set, and I just did what I had to without trying to think too much, like a tightrope walker focused on the platform at the end.

And I have to confess something: I did leave one thing out. I just couldn't bring myself to tell them about the kiss. Trust me, they're not ready for that. They might not ever be ready for that. And is it really their business? I mean, it was just a kiss—it's not like I sneaked out and got birth control or something.

If keeping that kiss to myself makes me a sinner, then I guess I'll just have to deal with it when I get to heaven. For now, I'm sticking with my decision.

When I was done, when I'd told them everything (except, you know), the three of us sat in silence for a while, exhausted. My father turned the car back on to roll down the windows. They'd gotten fogged up from our breath.

Finally my mother said in a sad voice, "I don't know what's happened to you, Mena. You used to be such a nice girl."

"God, Mom! I'm still nice!"

"Don't take the Lord's name in vain."

I almost started crying again.

"I don't know what we're going to do with you," she said. "But I can guarantee you're never seeing those Connors again."

Then I did cry. "Please, Mom! It's not their fault! I was just too afraid to tell you what was going on. It was all me—I swear. The Connors had nothing to do with it. They're really nice people. And Mrs. Connor is the greatest person. She's a widow. Casey's dad died when he was eleven. They're all still really sad."

Maybe that softened her some—I couldn't tell.

Because for the next ten minutes, my mother went through this whole History of Mena, reminiscing about what a good girl I used to be and how I used to make them so proud. You think it doesn't hurt to hear yourself talked about in the past that way?

"We never had to worry about you," she said. "We'd hear our friends complain about their kids, and we'd always think, 'Thank goodness—not our Mena.' And now."

"I'm sorry." I must have said that a hundred times since my father parked the car.

Finally my mother lost all her energy. It's like she'd given up—not just on the argument, but on me.

"So, Mena, tell me what we should do. If you were the mother, what would you do?"

What a terrible question. I hate to think how strict I'd be. I hate to think how furious I'd feel if someone had lied to me like that.

So I didn't think about it. It was too hard. Instead I took a chance.

"Can we start over?" I said. "Please?"

"And what exactly does that mean?"

I didn't plan what I'd say, I just said it. "I want to go to church—to another church. I miss it. I want to be good—I like being good. I'm not trying to suddenly turn bad. I want you—" I choked up. I had to wait a second to continue. "I want you to be proud of me again. That's all I ever wanted."

My mother didn't seem so angry anymore. Her eyes had softened at the creases. And even though my father still hadn't turned around this whole time, I could see part of his face in the rearview mirror, and I could tell I was getting to him.

"But you guys, I also want to have friends. The church kids—they're never going to be my friends again. I don't want them. They're too mean. I'm sorry, but that's the truth. And Casey—he's just such a nice person. And Kayla and her friends—"

I stopped before my mother felt the need to point out that Kayla and her friends had been part of the deception.

I'm trying to learn how to quit when I'm ahead—or at least when I'm not so far behind.

My mother sounded so tired. "Your father and I will talk about it."

Which I know means my mother will talk, my father will agree, and my mother will issue the sentence. Which is fine, as long as it's something I can live with. Please, no more house arrest.

I let them get out of the car first, and waited a little while before I followed. When I went upstairs, their bedroom door was closed—I assume so they could talk about me behind my back. Good. I was happy for the distraction.

I hurried downstairs and turned on the computer.

And typed the question that had been burning in me since church.

Fifty

MENA@REECEINSURANCE: What were you doing
there???

NUMENOR: I thought you might like some moral
support.

MENA@REECEINSURANCE: How did you know
where to go?

NUMENOR: I read the *Post*.

MENA@REECEINSURANCE: You nearly gave me a
heart attack.

NUMENOR: Sorry. Quite a performance that guy
gave. You okay?

MENA@REECEINSURANCE: Not sure yet.

NUMENOR: Anything I can do?

MENA@REECEINSURANCE: Smuggle me out of the
country.

NUMENOR: What's the temperature at home?

MENA@REECEINSURANCE: Frozen. Still waiting. My
parents are discussing me right now.

NUMENOR: Granted, I've only gone to church a few

times, but I don't remember the preacher ever pointing out anyone in the audience and suggesting they go hang themselves. Seems kind of harsh.

MENA@REECEINSURANCE: Tell me about it.

NUMENOR: Seriously, are you okay?

MENA@REECEINSURANCE: I think so. It was nice of you to come today. Sorry we couldn't talk.

NUMENOR: Hey, if you want, I could give you the name of that church—the non-hanging one. Maybe I'd even show up there again. You think if you met me there, your parents might actually let me see you? You know, see ;) you?

MENA@REECEINSURANCE: Fat chance until I'm 16. Would you really ever go to church?

NUMENOR: If there's a girl in it for me, sure.

MENA@REECEINSURANCE: That's not very pious.

NUMENOR: Josh took ballroom dancing with K. I'd say he had it far worse.

MENA@REECEINSURANCE: What church is it?

NUMENOR: The one where we had my dad's funeral. Ms. Shepherd told us about it. It's where she goes.

MENA@REECEINSURANCE: MS. SHEPHERD GOES TO CHURCH????

NUMENOR: Yep. Intriguing, no?

Fifty-one

I had to know.

The more I thought about it—not only what Casey had said, but what Ms. Shepherd said in class—I knew I had to ask.

It was when Teresa kept hounding her, pressing Ms. Shepherd to say what she believed.

The taxpayers of this community do not pay me to discuss my personal views. I share personal views on my own time.

Well, Sunday night is her own time, right?

And her website—that's her personal thing, too, right?

I waited until my parents were asleep. From what I've read on her blog, I know Ms. Shepherd is a night owl.

The big problem with my e-mail address is there's never any way to disguise who I am. Someday when I get an account of my own, I'm going to be DogLvr or Christmas-pup or something cuter—and more anonymous—than just my name.

MENA@REECEINSURANCE: Hi, Ms. Shepherd. I
    hope you don't mind me bothering you. Are
    you busy right now?

It didn't take long to get an answer.

BIOHAZARDESS: Semi. What can I do for you, Ms.
    Reece?

I sat there and drummed my fingers lightly on top of
the keys, stalling. I knew generally what I wanted to ask
her, but I wasn't sure how to start.

MENA@REECEINSURANCE: I was just wondering.
    You said in class that you share your personal
    views on your own time. I was wondering—
    does that include now?
BIOHAZARDESS: Now is fine.
MENA@REECEINSURANCE: Are you sure?
BIOHAZARDESS: I am now. I might not be in five
    seconds, so ask away.

With that kind of time pressure, I just blurted it out.

MENA@REECEINSURANCE: Do you believe
    in God?
BIOHAZARDESS: Yes.

My heart did a little jig.

MENA@REECEINSURANCE: And you also believe in
    evolution.
BIOHAZARDESS: You've been paying attention.
MENA@REECEINSURANCE: Then why don't you
    just say so in class? Then nobody would be
    upset.
BIOHAZARDESS: Except me. I would be gravely
    upset. I take the separation of church and state
    very seriously.
MENA@REECEINSURANCE: But if you just told them
    you're one of them, they wouldn't bother you
    anymore.
BIOHAZARDESS: Yes, they would. I'm not one
    of them. I believe in science. They want
    me to teach something that isn't science.
    I will never agree to that. That would be
    lying.
MENA@REECEINSURANCE: Then can you explain it
    to me? What do you believe?
BIOHAZARDESS: I believe that God created the
    universe and everything in it, and that
    evolution is the best explanation of what
    systems He used to effect it.
        Does that make sense?
MENA@REECEINSURANCE: Yes, I think so.
BIOHAZARDESS: Good. So let's start with some
    basics. As I hope I've conveyed in class, there
    is a natural order to the universe. It's beautiful
    in its simplicity and logic. Evolution is part

of that natural order. Evolution is simply true. There's nothing evil about it. With me so far?

MENA@REECEINSURANCE: Yes.

BIOHAZARDESS: Good. Now, quantum physics tells us that at the same time there's this beautiful, perfect order to all things in a very large sense, there is also a part of our universe—down at the smallest level—that will never EVER be predictable. There are just some things we cannot control. Still with me?

MENA@REECEINSURANCE: I think so. It's like all that weird stuff you were saying to Josh.

BIOHAZARDESS: Correct. What it means, in a nutshell, is this: The future is not set. Which tells me there will always be room for the miraculous. God left Himself some slack in the rope. As a scientist, I may try to know everything about this universe there is to know, but even then I will never be able to touch that part—that mystery—that lies at the heart of all things.

To me, that's where God is. And it's also proof that I have free will. If the future isn't set, I can affect my course. My prayers can matter. How I live my life matters. I'm not just some computer living out my program.

That is the God I believe in. It's the God

who created a universe so vast and wonderful
for me to explore and test and observe, and yet
I have the pleasure of knowing some mysteries
will have to wait until I can ask Him face to
face.

Does that answer your question?

I sat back and looked at the screen and tried to let her words settle in my brain. To be honest, I'm not sure I got it all. But the part about there being something unpredictable about the universe—that I can believe. And the idea that that's where God is—I think I understand that, too.

I wanted to take more time to let it sink in, but I also didn't want to leave Ms. Shepherd hanging.

MENA@REECEINSURANCE: I think I understand, but
can I ask you one more question?
BIOHAZARDESS: Yes.
MENA@REECEINSURANCE: I still don't get why you
don't just tell them you're on their side. I mean,
just to make peace?
BIOHAZARDESS: Because I'm not on their side and
they're not on mine. Their side wants me to
pretend the facts are not what they are.
Intelligent design is not science. In fact, it's
hostile to science—it tells people not to believe
what science has proven to be true. And at a
time like this, we need more young people like
you to pursue science as a career so you can

tell us all the things we don't know yet. I can't allow anyone to discourage that.

MENA@REECEINSURANCE: But what if a new school board gets in and won't let you teach evolution anymore? What are you going to do then?

BIOHAZARDESS: I believe in God. I believe in evolution. I believe in the separation of church and state. Which one of those should I lie about just to make peace?

Fifty-two

I decided not to wait until senior year. I took an early bus and got off a few blocks from school and stopped to make my purchase. I kept it safe in my locker until third period.

I brought in my offering and laid it on Ms. Shepherd's desk and sat down without ever making eye contact. I figure what makes Josh so cool is he is a man of few words—plus, he has amazing computer and T-shirt design skills, but I'll shoot for one out of three.

Ms. Shepherd opened the brown and orange paper bag and set the pumpkin scone on top. She broke off a corner, popped it in her mouth, closed her eyes, and savored it. Josh was a little slow with the coffee today. Ms. Shepherd had almost finished the scone before she had something to wash it down with.

We didn't make eye contact at all, Ms. Shepherd and I. And that was fine with me. I was feeling a little shy around her, both because of our conversation last night and because of what Kayla told me this morning.

Casey and I ran into her as we left the library right before first period. I'm sure I was looking guilty, but Kayla didn't pick up on it. Her mind was already on the next issue of the *Post*. She was on her way to a meeting with her reporters.

She wore a T-shirt I hadn't seen yet—*Brainiacs Unite*. "Josh just made it yesterday," Kayla said, reaching over to fluff up Casey's hair. "I'll get you both one. I'd say you qualify."

She caught us up on the current stats. "Eight thousand visitors a day and counting. We're getting a lot of play off other bloggers' links—science, religion, politics. People love you, Bible Grrr—"

I shushed her and looked around to make sure no one had heard.

Kayla ignored my paranoia. "I think a lot of the traffic is coming off Ms. Shepherd's site. That was bound to give us a boost—her numbers are huge. So if she says you're golden, you're golden."

"She doesn't . . . know about me, does she?"

"Your secret identity? 'Course she does. Knew it before she linked."

"Kayla!"

"Inner circle, baby. I told ya." She fluffed Casey's hair one more time and was off to stir up more trouble.

How weird. Ms. Shepherd knew Bible Grrrl was me—just some freshman girl in one of her classes, who isn't even that great at science—and yet she still linked to me off her website. Why? She knows far more than I do—about God, about science, about everything. So why is she linking to me?

But maybe the thing is she can't do everything. She's handling the science end of things, and maybe it's up to Bible Grrrl to handle the Bible. Not that I'm so great at that, either, but I'm willing to keep trying. I told my parents about it during that whole big confessional, and that was the one thing they actually liked. Which is good, because I have a plan.

You know how Kayla said that thing on her blog about me coming up with a whole Universal Theory of Religion and Science? I know she was probably just kidding, but I actually think it's a great idea. I'd like to figure out how to explain things in a way that would make someone like Bethany Wells believe in someone like Ms. Shepherd. It would be like my gift to humanity.

Maybe I should ask Ms. Shepherd if I can make that my science project. She'll probably say no, since it's not strictly SCIENCE, but I should ask anyway. I'm going to need a new project no matter what, since I don't feel right about taking credit for Casey's. Most of those ideas were his. I just did some puppy wrangling and some graphing, and even though I did come up with a few experiments on my own, it's nothing compared to Casey's effort. Besides, I would have done all that whether or not it meant an A plus plus in the class, since I can honestly say those were the happiest days of my life. So far. Especially last Friday night.

And anyway, wouldn't it be nice to see Casey win his place on Ms. Shepherd's website all by himself? I feel kind of weird I beat him to it.

Speaking of Casey, there's this spot in the back of the library where if you duck down behind the last carrel and are super quick about it, you can actually kiss your boyfriend without anyone ever knowing. It's not even close to being as great as sitting in a dark room with the scent of puppy in the air, but right now I'll take what I can get.

And did you notice that? *Boyfriend*. Not just boy friend. I think I know the difference.

And my last piece of good news: my parents said we're switching churches. Not that it was that big of a surprise, considering what happened, but I was still thrilled when they told me. They haven't decided where we'll go next. Maybe Ms. Shepherd's church? I'm not going to push it. But wouldn't that be cool? Not going to push it.

As hard as it was to tell my parents the truth about all my lies, it hasn't turned out that badly. The telling was the hardest part. I'm still on restriction for the next few months, but at least I don't have to worry about them finding anything out. I wasn't meant for sneaking around. Teresa was always better at that than I was.

Speaking of Teresa, I've been thinking about what Ms. Shepherd said—about how it's the freaks of nature who survive. And looking at my life these past few months in scientific terms, I can see how clearly she's right.

This is how I view it: I've spent years with Teresa and the other church kids, perfectly content to be part of their species. I saw no reason to change. Then something happened—Denny Pierce happened—and something inside me started to mutate. It's been painful to shed my skin or grow gills or whatever you want to call it, but now here I am, this new creature, and I don't fit with my old species anymore.

If you look at it strictly scientifically, it doesn't mean I'm good and they're bad or vice versa. It just means we're different. Teresa is one kind of freak of nature, I'm another, Denny Pierce is one, Casey and Kayla and Ms. Shepherd are others. All of us out here mutating and adapting and doing our best to survive.

Maybe some of my old friends will want to be like me someday. Maybe not. Like Ms. Shepherd said, there's room for the miraculous. Maybe Teresa will grow horns.

But I've decided that from now on, I'm just going to go forward and be what I am. Stop looking back and wondering what went wrong. Nothing went wrong. This is how it's supposed to be.

In a way, I get to be like one of Abbey's puppies. Setting off on my new life, with my basket of pigs' ears and a brand-new squeaky toy. It's hard to leave the backyard and the rest of the litter behind, but that doesn't mean my new life will be any less fun. In fact, it might be better than I could ever imagine.

I'm proud to be a freak of nature. It's what's gotten me this far.

I think I'll tell that to Josh. Maybe he'll put it on a T-shirt.

Acknowledgments

As I have to remind myself when I notice the day is half gone and I still haven't settled down to work, books don't just write themselves. This one was no exception. I am deeply grateful for the assistance, input, and talents of the following people:

High school teachers Shannon Koza, Marisu McNamara, and Peggy Woods. Thank you to Ms. Koza in particular for letting me sit in on so many of your freshman biology classes and never calling on me once.

Dr. Kenneth R. Miller, professor of biology at Brown University and author of *Finding Darwin's God: A Scientist's Search for Common Ground Between God and Evolution*. Thank you for your time and advice, and for setting such a fine example of how to be a person of both faith and science.

Ellen, Randy, Casey, and Connor Clark for raising such wonderful test subjects. Thank you to Casey in particular for the kiss that launched the subplot.

Carolyn Sweeney, for letting me e-mail her this novel as I wrote it each day, and always responding, "Send me more!" It absolutely kept me going. Thank you also for spending so many hours with me on the phone reviewing the many joys and outrages of our high school days together to make sure I got them right, and for providing me with valuable insight from your own years of teaching high school.

Author Barry Lyga for always pushing both of us to do better and better work, and for reading, editing, and rereading every story that's come out of my fingers for the last several years. My work is so much richer because of you. And thanks for never letting me forget that I once asked you how often *Publishers Weekly* comes out. Get over it. I was tired.

Authors Dean Wesley Smith and Kristine Kathryn Rusch for being so generous with their time, and for sharing the advice that changed my life and helped me understand writing as a career.

The supremely talented, high-class team at Knopf and Random House, including but not limited to Michelle Frey, Nancy Hinkel, Michele Burke, and Melanie Chang. Thank you to Michelle Frey in particular for exceeding any wish I've ever had about an editor. You're brilliant and clever and kind, and I could gush all day.

My agent, Laura Rennert, for all her hard work and valuable counsel, and for her expert matchmaking skills. I appreciate all your efforts now and in the future.

And finally, my husband (you know who you are), for making it possible for me to write this novel in the first place by supporting me in every known sense of the word. Thanks for kissing me and getting me fired. It's all been puppies and flowers since then.